INCANTATION

LITTLE, BROWN AND COMPANY

New York ᛊ Boston

Alice Hoffman

INCANTATION

Little, Brown and Company

Hachette Book Group USA
1271 Avenue of the Americas, New York, NY 10020
Visit our Web site at www.lb-teens.com

First Edition: October 2006

Library of Congress Cataloging-in-Publication Data

Hoffman, Alice.
    Incantation / by Alice Hoffman. — 1st ed.
        p. cm.
    Summary: During the Spanish Inquisition, sixteen-year-old Estrella,
brought up a Catholic, discovers her family's true Jewish identity, and when
their secret is betrayed by Estrella's best friend, the consequences are tragic.
    ISBN-13: 978-0-316-01019-1 (hardcover)
    ISBN-10: 0-316-01019-7 (hardcover)
    [1. Prejudices—Fiction. 2. Identity—Fiction. 3. Marranos—Fiction.
4. Inquisition—Spain—Fiction.] I. Title.
PZ7.H67445Hy 2006
    [Fic]—dc22   2005037301

10 9 8 7 6 5 4 3 2 1

RRD-C
Printed in the United States of America

Book design by Alyssa Morris
The text was set in Sabellicus, and the display type is Telegdi Antique.

I thought I knew the world.

I thought I knew myself.

I thought I knew my dearest friend.

But I knew nothing at all.

—Estrella deMadrigal
Spain 1500

SOUL

Be careful

Ashes

If every life is a river, then it's little wonder that we do not even notice the changes that occur until we are far out in the darkest sea. One day you look around and nothing is familiar, not even your own face.

My name once meant *daughter, granddaughter, friend, sister, beloved.* Now those words mean only what their letters spell out: Star in the night sky. Truth in the darkness.

I have crossed over to a place where I never thought I'd be. I am someone I would have never imagined. A secret. A dream. I am this, body and soul. Burn me. Drown me. Tell me lies. I will still be who I am.

WE LIVED in a tiny village in Spain. It is gone now, but then it was called Encaleflora, the name of the lime flower, something bitter and something sweet mixed into one. It was a town that had been my family's home for more than five hundred years, a beautiful village in the most beautiful countryside in all of Aragon.

It began on a hot day.

I was out in the garden when I smelled something burning. Not lime flowers, only pure bitterness. Cores, rinds, pits. That was the way it started. That was the way our world disappeared.

ON THE DAY of the burning, my dearest friend, Catalina, ran into our yard and grabbed my hand, urging me to follow her.

Let's run to the Plaza, Catalina said. *Let's see what's on fire.*

Catalina was always curious, always fun. She had a laugh that reminded me of the sound of water. She was shorter than I, but even though my grandmother said Catalina's hair was too curly and her nose was bumpy, I thought we looked like sisters.

Catalina and I were so close nothing could come between us. We had been best friends from the time we were babies. When I looked at my friend I saw not only the child she'd been and the girl that she was, but also the woman she was about to be. Other girls I knew talked behind your back and smiled at you falsely. Not Catalina. She knew who I was deep inside: I could be lazy sometimes; I believed in true love; I was head-strong and loyal, a friend until the end of time.

Because of our jet-colored hair, Catalina and I had been given similar pet names as little girls. I had been called Raven and Catalina had been Crow. Our birthdays were one week apart, and we had at last turned sixteen. We thought about our futures, how they twined around each other, as if we were two strands of a single braid of fate. Even when we were married women, we planned to live next door to each other. We thought we knew exactly what our lives were made of: still water, not a moving river.

We thought nothing would ever change.

ON THE BURNING DAY, we raced down to the Plaza, where we always went to fetch water. There was a well in the center of the Plaza, and the water we pulled up in wooden buckets was said to come from heaven. It was sweet and clear and so cold it made us shiver.

To the north stood the old Duke's palace, but he was gone, and our church council reported directly to the king, Ferdinand. The palace was empty, except for the soldiers' barracks and the center where letters could be posted. People said the ghost of the Duke came down to drink cold, clear water on windy nights and that you could hear him if you listened carefully. But today no one was drawing water from the well, not even a ghost. There were scores of men all around, but they hadn't come for water. Soldiers had built a pyre out of aged wood. Pine and old forest oak, all of it so dry it burst into flames the moment a lit torch touched the wood.

At first I thought the soldiers were burning

doves. White things were rising into the sky. I felt so sad for those poor burning birds, then I realized the burning pile was made of books. Pages flew upward, disappearing, turning to embers and ash, drifting into nothingness.

I saw a man with a red circle on his coat, crying. He had a long beard like my grandfather, but my grandfather would never cry, with tears streaming down his beard, there for all to see. The crying man was begging the soldiers not to throw his books on the fire, and they were laughing at him. A guard took a handful of ashes and tossed them onto the old man so that sparks flared all over his coat.

He's from the alajama, Catalina whispered about the old man.

That was the part of town where Jews lived that some called the *juderia*. Our parents didn't allow us to go there. We were Christians. A hundred years beforehand most of the Jews in Spain had either been forced to convert or flee the country. The stubborn ones who remained and declared themselves to be Jews were the ones who lived behind gates—the red circle people who seemed willing to do anything, even die, for their precious books; people who by law could not own land, marry outside their faith, eat a meal with a Christian.

There were cinders floating down into Catalina's black hair. She didn't notice, so I brushed them away.

Those are his books, Catalina said of the old man in the ashes. *The town council has posted a new decree. No Jewish books, no medical books, no magic books.*

I saw the way the soldiers treated this man. As if he were a bird caught in a snare made of his own bones. His coat had caught on fire, but he no longer cried. I think he may have looked at me. I think I may have looked back.

Catalina applauded with the other onlookers in the square when a soldier threw a bucket of cold water over the old man. I merely stood there.

My mother, Abra, had taught me that all people are made from the same dust. When our days here are gone, all men and women enter the same garden. My mother had put a finger to her lips when she told me this. She taught me some of what she'd learned from her father, secret things I must never repeat. Lessons that sounded as though they would be easy, but which turned out to be difficult. How to look at stars and know their names. How to gaze into a bowl of water until it was possible to see all that existed in that one small bowl.

Once I fell asleep while gazing, and my mother laughed when I awoke with a start, my chin in the water.

I'm not smart enough to learn anything, I had admitted.

You don't learn such things, my mother had said. *You feel them.*

Now my mother saw me with Catalina in the Plaza. She looked shocked to see us in the middle of the rioting, in a place we shouldn't be.

My mother had a basket of wool with her; she had been to the dye vats near the river, and her arms were tinted from her work. My mother was known for the yarn she sold. Whatever Abra did was beautiful; she had the ability to make something wondrous out of something plain. That was her talent, one I envied. Any wool spun at her wheel was finer than all the rest, even though our sheep were as silly as any others.

Sometimes I went with my mother when she called on her clients, carrying a basket of yarn that was dyed every shade of blue imaginable. Turquoise, aqua, night blue, ultramarine, bird's egg blue, early morning blue, inside-of-a-cloud blue, pond blue, river blue, blue as all eternity. My mother's hands were always blue, sometimes like water, sometimes like the sky, sometimes like the colors of a bird's feathers.

There in the Plaza, my mother was like a piece of the sky coming right at me. A person should never come face-to-face with the sky. She looked as frightening as my grandmother did when she was angry. Fierce. Unrelenting. She ran over and grabbed me. There must have been sparks in my hair as there had been in Catalina's, because my mother put her hands in my hair. She clasped my head so hard that it hurt.

My mother and I had always been more like sisters than mother and daughter, but not today. Today I was a child, one who should have known better than to be in the Plaza. Without waiting for me to explain, my mother dragged me along, tugging on my hair. My black hair that was so long I sometimes felt I had wings. Even before the other children called me Raven, I had often dreamed I could fly. I would fly until I could go no farther, so far away no one had ever been there before. In my dreams I would enter into a garden where the roses were big enough for me to curl up inside them. I would know how to decipher symbols I had never even seen in my waking life.

As we left the Plaza, I looked over my shoulder. The man with the red circle was curled up as the guards kicked him. There were no roses, only the brightness of the flames. Ashes kept falling. The Plaza was dirty and gray.

Something from deep inside the world had crept up from the well; a monster set loose in our midst. The fire was his breath; the jeers all around were his snarls. I felt something burn inside of me.

I called for Catalina, but she was too busy watching the guards to pay any attention. My mother refused to let me stay alongside my friend.

We are leaving and that's that. Never look at other people's bad fortune, my mother said. *If you do, it will come back to find you instead of its rightful owner.*

Bones

All that day we could hear people shouting in the streets. Stones were thrown; windows were smashed; the gates of the juderia were painted red, the color of the devil's work. In edicts posted all over the village, the town fathers declared they were sick of the Jews stealing from them, although what had been stolen was never disclosed.

Because some Jews were moneylenders, they were blamed for the town's recent bad fortune. In truth, everyone knew Jews were only permitted to lend money because the church wouldn't allow one Christian to lend another money. How much money could there be in such dealings? The Jews weren't rich. In the walled-off section of town where they lived, there were no lime trees, no ivy, no gardens filled with jasmine. In summer, the heat baked the bare earth into bricks. I had seen the children looking through the wall; they wore no shoes. At night, the gate was locked, the way we locked the pens of our chickens and pigs.

People came to ask my grandfather, Jose deMadrigal, what he thought of what was happening in the Plaza. Our closest friends always wanted his advice. My grandfather was a respected teacher. Boys in the village often came to study with him; only the best students, the brightest boys. These students were afraid of my grandfather, as I was, but there was something more in these boys' eyes: they admired him. They hurried to their lessons and bowed when my grandfather walked in the door. They huddled around him to hear his wisdom, just as our friends did on the day of the burning.

My older brother, Luis, was studying at the seminary. He was my grandparents' favorite, and for good reason. Luis was compassionate and kind, a brilliant student. Being at the seminary was an honor, and Luis had passed many difficult exams before he was chosen. My grandfather had helped him in his studies toward becoming a priest; he'd worked hard with Luis, teaching him Latin and Greek. I often heard my grandfather say a prayer for my brother when he thought no one could hear, not like the ones we said in church; something special, for Luis alone.

No matter how proud I was, I missed my brother, especially today, when everything seemed so frightening. I knew we'd all feel better if Luis were at home.

As for me, to the great Jose deMadrigal I was nothing more than a bothersome fly, not worth the least bit of attention. I was jealous, because my grandfather ignored me even when I asked the simplest questions: Why did we light candles on some nights and not others? Why couldn't girls be educated?

Take the child away, he would call to my grandmother whenever I questioned him. *Teach her to make bread.*

He felt that way about all women, except for my mother, whom he treated as though she were a son. He adored Abra, and because of this my mother thought she was the queen of all fate. My grandfather had let her run wild, so my mother was not afraid of anything or anyone. She could speak so many languages, people joked that she could speak to the birds. She was so intelligent that when my grandfather's friends came over for tea and heated discussions, my grandfather let her participate in the conversations. Women were not often allowed to do this. Abra had to sit behind a screen at these times. Otherwise men who were scholars might stop thinking about serious matters; one of them might even get it into his head that he should marry my mother.

Abra considered herself married for all eternity — even though my father, the love of her life, had been gone for so long. He was lost to illness when I was only a baby, in the time of the black fever. He left us before I could remember him. But I remembered how much my mother loved him. She still wore an emerald ring my father had given to her on their wedding day. She was partial to emeralds; she said they were the single thing that remained constant, always green, always the same.

WHEN OUR FRIENDS gathered in our doorway on the burning day, my grandfather told them that the soldiers in the Plaza were driven by bloodlust and evil. A monster brought to life, just as I'd thought. Something let loose from the very deepest part of the earth.

Stay away, my grandfather told our friends. *You don't fight a monster with sticks and stones.*

Even the pigs in the yard were frightened by the noise in the Plaza. Poor Dini, my special pet, hid under the porch. Other families killed a pig every spring to make chorizo sausages, but my family preferred green vegetables, so Dini was getting strong and fat. Catalina and I often sneaked him into my room and let him sleep on my bed while we played with him as if he were a doll. Once we dressed him up in my brother's baby clothes. When I called Dini by name he came running to me, and he would bow on command.

All the same, Dini was still a big baby, afraid of the screaming in the Plaza, refusing to come out from under the porch, even when called, which meant I would have to wash him later with lavender soap so my grandmother wouldn't complain that he was a filthy creature that should be sold at market.

My grandfather may have ignored me completely, but my grandmother was even worse. She noticed only what was wrong, never what was right. My grandmother was called Carmen, but I never thought of her as a woman with a name. She was too demanding for anything as human as that. I called her *Señora* out of respect, but also out of fear.

My grandmother had long white hair that she braided and wore up, like most women her age. She knew all the tricks a girl might play, and she couldn't abide laziness. Sometimes I truly believed my grandmother could read the thoughts in my head, especially if they were thoughts of doing bad things, like climbing out the window at night to sneak through the Arrias family's yard and meet Catalina so that we could dance in the field of sunflowers when the moon was high in the sky. My grandmother would always be waiting outside the window, ready to catch me when I came back. As a punishment I would have to sweep not just the house, but also the yard where the chickens were kept.

Sometimes the little Arrias sisters from next door, Marianna and Antonia, came to help me with my chores while their mother was out cutting sunflowers for the market. All the while we worked, my grandmother would watch with a tight, unfriendly smile. *See,* she was telling me without saying a word. *Even the little sisters do better than you, and they are only eight and nine.* She would offer the Arrias sisters drinks of iced lime, *alicante granizado,* or *horchata,* almond milk, treats she never offered to me.

Nothing I did was good enough for my grandmother. When she taught me to make *kouclas,* the dumplings we added to our favorite dish, *adafina,* our Friday night chicken stew, she would stand right over me. *Mix it faster,* she would say.

Any dumpling I tried to make always fell apart. Unlike my mother, I did not make things more beautiful. Under my grandmother's watchful eyes, I grew nervous and made mistakes.

Don't cut your nails and let them fall! my

grandmother would tell me. *That is a sure way to be cursed.* She would gather my nail clippings together and burn them in a dish till they were nothing but ash. She said she wanted to protect me from any *echizo,* witchcraft; witches made spells out of nails and hair.

Once I used rouge before going to church on Sunday, and although I swore that the sun had burned me, my grandmother scrubbed my face with soap.

You'll bring a curse on us, she vowed.

It was little wonder I spent as much time as I could next door. On one side of our house was the Arriases' cottage, on the other side lived Catalina's family. Catalina's home was not as clean as ours, or as well kept. There were no silver candlesticks or good linens; still I preferred it. Catalina's mother gave us almond cakes without our even asking. Catalina's mother told me I had nimble fingers on days she taught us needlepoint. When I helped her with chores, she swore she couldn't have asked for a more helpful girl. Once when Catalina was not in the room, her mother sighed and told me she wished Catalina were as pretty as I.

I laughed and said, *But she is! We look just like sisters.*

Catalina's father was a quiet man, a cobbler who sat beside a pile of boots. He was easygoing and never raised his voice the way my grandfather did, but Catalina looked down on him. A man who fixed other people's shoes was worthless, she said. Catalina would someday marry her cousin Andres, who had come to live with her family when his own parents died of fever, and Catalina had high hopes for him.

Andres is smart, Caterina told me. *He'll take my father's olive grove and make us rich.*

On the evening of the burning in the Plaza, I started to go to Catalina's house, but my grandmother came after me. Maybe one of the reasons I spent so much time at Catalina's was because of Andres. We both had parents who had died, and we often talked about that, how you don't forget such things, even if you don't exactly remember.

But going next door was impossible now. My grandmother had pulled me aside, into the yard where we grew grapes. After all those ashes in the air, the vines smelled sweet.

Your grandfather and I bought something for you on the day you were born, my grandmother said. *On a day when there's fire, there should also be water. You're sixteen now. You're old enough.*

I was stunned when she showed me a perfect strand of pearls. When my grandmother fastened them around my throat, I didn't know what to say. I wasn't used to her kindness.

The pearls were indeed as cold as water, but after a moment they warmed to my skin.

These were always meant for you, little Esther, my grandmother said. I was even more stunned to have her call me by this special name that my mother had used for me long ago, when she sang me lullabies.

Sometimes my grandfather called my grandmother by a special name, one my mother said I should never repeat. The secret name sounded like glass, something broken and strange. My mother had laughed when I once gave her my impression of my grandfather calling for my grandmother. I sounded as if I were choking.

That's the way love sounds, my mother told me. *You think it should feel like honey, but instead it cuts like a knife.*

I was beginning to understand. My grandmother's love was cold because she was afraid of things; that was why everything had to be perfect. I bowed my head and thanked her for her gift. Then, before I could stop myself, I threw my arms around her. The pearls were my treasure and my truth, and I would only wear them on special days. The most important days of my life.

THE NEXT MORNING, I was so deeply asleep that my mother had to shake me awake so that we could go to shop in the Muslim quarter. In the middle of the night I had heard men talking in my grandfather's study under the stairs in the cellar; they were gathered in a room where I wasn't allowed. Their conversations ran together into a chant that filtered through my sleep. In my dreams, I had walked through a gate. I often dreamed this, and my mother told me this was an unusual dream. It was a dream that some people never had, not if they stared into still water for days or weeks, not if they studied with the greatest teachers.

What did the gate look like? My mother asked

me that morning. *Was it made of gold or marble or emeralds? Was your father in the garden?*

I didn't want to disappoint my mother and tell her the truth: The gate in my dream had been made out of bones. I didn't want to tell her that even though I'd had this dream many times, even though the garden was always the same, the gate was always different. In every dream I had no idea where I was. I was lost, unable to call out or find my own way. The only thing that remained the same was the garden, lush and emerald green.

WE WERE NOT allowed to go into the alajama—for that, you needed to be a person marked with a red circle—but we could go to the Muslim part of town, which was on the outskirts, since the *Mudejars,* like the Jews, were not allowed to live side-by-side with Christians.

Abra fully understood their chatter, a mix of Spanish and Arabic, and could converse with the storekeepers while bargaining for cinnamon and cloves and sweet blood oranges, which were red in the center, like a heart. In the Muslim stores there were enameled teapots, ceramic tiles, silk from Arabia spun by a thousand worms, candy made of sesame seeds and honey, copper bowls hammered with patterns that were so intricate there was no beginning and no end to their design.

WE WENT OUT of our way to make one special visit whenever we went to the quarter. The wife of a Muslim doctor who always bought yarn from my mother was also kind enough to offer us cups of mint tea when we came into her garden. There was a red lily that grew there, which my mother said could only be found in this one place. It was a miracle lily, one that grew from true devotion. This Muslim woman loved her husband as much as my mother had loved my father. The doctor's wife's perfect love had turned the lily red when she planted it in the ground and said a blessing over it; now it was one of a kind.

The doctor's wife needed yarn because she was making her husband a coat. Something he would be safe in; something that would last. She and my mother looked at each other as though they knew each other well. Certainly, they both knew we lived in a time when anyone could become an outcast, suddenly and without notice.

On this day, the doctor came to the window while my mother and his wife were searching through the baskets for the perfect skein of yarn. The doctor was tall and quiet; a handsome, educated man. Some Christians didn't believe in the medicines he used; all the same, when they were ill they often came to him for help.

His wife turned to him when he called a greeting to her; she held up some of the wool she had chosen and said something in a mix of Spanish and Arabic.

What did she say? I asked my mother.

She said, "The yarn woman has brought me something to help you fly, should you ever need to do so." *She said that's why she's making his coat the same color as the sky, so he can blend in and never be seen if he needs to escape from Encaleflora.*

I thought this was because there was talk in town of casting out any Muslim who wouldn't convert to Christianity—exactly what had been done to the Jews all those years ago. They called the Muslim converts *Moriscos,* but like most *Conversos,* they still weren't considered equals.

As we were walking home, my mother told me that love was the same in any language. She told me what the doctor's response to his wife had been, words that had nearly brought my mother to tears.

Fly away and leave you? Never.

The doctor's wife was sick with something her husband couldn't cure despite all his medicines. My mother was not a doctor, but she healed with herbs and spices and chanting. She was known for her skills, just as she was known for her beautiful yarn. She could take a spider's web and bind a sore so it wouldn't become puffy and green. She knew which mushrooms in the woods were good to eat and which ones caused aches or blindness or even death. For the doctor's wife, my mother had once made an amulet out of yarn and wood; the doctor's wife had slept with it beneath her pallet, but it had done nothing to cure her. Abra had also given the doctor's wife a canister of honey lavender tea that helped most ailing people with their appetite, but every time we went to the quarter, the doctor's wife was thinner, she was just a shadow of her-self waiting for my mother in the yard, beside the red lily.

My mother was a great healer, but there were mysteries that meant a closed door, even to Abra.

When nothing helped the doctor's wife, the one thing left to do was ask fate what would happen. When we got home from the quarter that day, my mother took out her cards. She kept them tied in a piece of blue silk that she stored beneath the pallet on her bed. The cards smelled like cinnabar, the perfume Abra used. They had odd letters on them, and those letters told the future.

The future of the Muslim doctor's wife made my mother her put her cards away for a long time.

Grass

I looked forward to going into the hills with my mother to help her collect whatever plants she needed. We tried to go at the beginning of each lunar month at a time my mother called by a secret name — *Rosh Hodesh,* the time of hope and possibility. As we searched in the meadows, she told me I must respect everything that grew. Some herbs were beautiful, they flowered and could heal, but their roots might be poisonous.

We collected different ingredients — some Abra would use for healing, others would be brought to the dying vats to change the color of the wool. Even a tiny addition would show in the yarn. A streak of tall grass or wildflower or seed could change everything. We collected bluebells, dark mushrooms that turned midnight-colored when soaked in water, the bark of the elder that is blue only at the core, inky reeds that grew by a pond, green grasses whose husks were blue-black. There was one beautiful plant we avoided; it had a red flower, similar to the one in the doctor's wife's garden, but if you touched this flower, blisters would form on your skin as though you were burning.

My mother was teaching me that the inside of something was not necessarily its outside.

Always look carefully, she told me. *Look with more than your eyes.*

When I told my mother of the pearls my grandmother had given me, she told me that on the day I was born my grandparents went to a town far away. They bought the pearls from a man who went halfway around the world, to waters we'd never heard of and would never see, a place where the most perfect pearls could be found.

It's more than a necklace, my mother said. *Look carefully at that gift and you'll see what you mean to your grandmother.*

That was one of the reasons I loved to go to the hills with my mother; she talked to me in a different way, as though she weren't a mother, or a friend, but a teacher, one in possession of every-thing I would ever need to know.

What do you and your mother do up in the hills? my friend Catalina had asked me. *Some people say there are witches up there.*

I laughed. Catalina could be such a child. *We look for blue things,* I told her. *We find whatever is beautiful and what can be used to heal.*

Whenever we had filled our baskets, my mother and I often went to a place on the hilltop. From here we could gaze at our whole town, spread out before us; at this distance the village seemed tiny enough to fit in a pocket. Everything we cared about was down there, but my mother always stared at the sky. I thought she was remembering my father when she did this. I thought she could see his face somehow, in the shapes of the clouds.

That blue is the color of tears, she said.

Tears are clear, I told her.

My mother shook her head. She was my age doubled with three extra years. She knew more than I would even if I lived until the age of one hundred.

You haven't looked closely enough. Tears are exactly that color. Blue.

My mother told me things that were not part of what her father had taught her. This was a different path altogether. She said, *Women know things that men will never know. We keep the best secrets. We tell the best stories.*

Late at night, when my grandparents were asleep, I would sit with my mother on her bed and listen to more of what she knew. I learned the cures for headaches and the cure for dreams. Lavender, coriander, green onions, lime juice, and licorice. Rue, garlic, ginger. Simple things that were surprisingly strong when mixed together in the right combination.

I learned that on Friday nights the candles must be lit exactly at sundown and that healing was best at Rosh Hodesh, when the month was new and fresh. I learned to recite the prayers. *We praise you, eternal God.*

My mother taught me so much as we walked through the hills and then as we talked late at night. But most important of all, she explained that it was all right to say *No. I disagree.* That was a gift. I understood it was power. The power to think my own thoughts. The power to believe in myself.

Heart

During that summer, whenever our chores were through, Catalina and I would often sit in her yard, in the shade of an olive tree. The season was hot and dreamy; it seemed it would last forever. We would talk and watch Catalina's cousin Andres work in the fields beyond our houses. I couldn't stop staring at him. It had always been that way, but now it was worse. I looked and looked as though I were some foolish, mindless girl. I knew he and Catalina would marry someday. That had always been what her family had planned since they first took him into their household.

All the same, I kept looking.

There were almond trees out farther in the fields, and their scent made me dizzy.

I wish I lived with you, I told Catalina.

You should move in with us. Then we would be together all day every day.

It was an idle day made for idle thoughts. We planned our future, down to the meals we would cook. Catalina's favorite meal was spicy sausage; mine was rice with saffron and olive oil. We both liked pudding made of milk and almonds and sugar, and dark red wine whenever we could sneak a sip. We were making ourselves hungry and giddy. We had started to think of names for our children. Catalina would call her son Juan. I would call my daughter Angelina, little angel, a girl who does everything right and has none of my faults, someone who could please even my grandmother.

What is that you have? Catalina asked suddenly.

I had worn my pearls again, underneath my scarf. I knew I should put them in my treasure box under my bed, saved for important days. I had planned to do so, but they were so cool against my skin.

My grandmother gave these to me. They're only for special occasions.

Is today so special?

I felt uncomfortable, as though I had something I had no right to have.

I just wanted to show them to you, I said.

It wasn't exactly the truth, but it wasn't a lie either.

When you and Andres have a daughter, you can buy her pearls, I told Catalina.

I want rubies. Catalina laughed.

While we were talking, Andres called for water. Catalina said he was lazy. She liked to tease her cousin and boss him around. *Let him come here and get it for himself,* Catalina said, but I'd been emboldened by all our silliness and plans for what was to come. My pearls made me feel like a woman and not just a girl. I forgot myself and my place. I ran out to the field with a flask.

Soil rose up and dusted my face, and Andres leaned over and ran his hand over my forehead. I felt so hot I nearly drank the water myself.

What are you and Catalina plotting, Raven? Andres asked me.

People had stopped calling me that long ago. It was a child's name, but in Andres's mouth, it was something more. I was surprised to find he was looking at me in a way I hadn't expected. I wondered if the word Raven stuck in his throat like a knife.

Andres looked like an angel even though he had been digging in the field all day. His hair was long and pale. His eyes were blue. He was so unusual, so handsome, that people always stopped and stared at him, as I now did.

Your cousin thinks I should move in with you.

I couldn't believe the nerve I had. I let it sound as if it would just be the two of us. Me and Andres. Together. As if we were husband and wife. Catalina hadn't said it that way. She was the one with plans for Andres.

Andres laughed so hard he spit out the water he'd drank. Then he looked at me in another way.

Does she? And what do you say?

I say you're drooling.

I laughed and ran away. That was probably the reason my heart hurt so much. I ran so fast. All the same, even without looking, I could feel Andres watching me.

I was the exact same age my mother had been when she'd met my father and promised herself to him. I could smell almond flowers, and the heat crackled the air. When I narrowed my eyes and tried to see into my own future, all I could see was the white brightness of the sun. My throat hurt, not because of what I'd said, but because I had more words that I was afraid to say. I had wanted to shout out: *Yes! I say yes!* Instead I had run away.

What's wrong with my cousin? Catalina asked when I came back to sit beside her under the olive tree. *He has a foolish look on his face. You shouldn't have spoiled him and given him what he wanted. You have to teach boys how to behave.*

Andres was standing in the field when he should have been working on the irrigation ditch. My mother could never match the blue of his eyes with any of her colors, not if she tried for a thousand years. Bluebell, water reed, wild grass, feathers, none came close. It was as though I was in a dream. I couldn't see anything else but Andres, even from this distance, even though I knew he wasn't mine.

Are you still staring at him? Catalina asked.

Of course not, I said to my best friend.

And just like that, it was done. It was the first time I'd lied to her.

But it would not be the last.

WHEN LUIS came home from the seminary we celebrated, even though he would only be with us for one short week before he had to return to his studies. Luis took a coach from Barcelona, then walked from the Plaza. All of our neighbors went out to their verandas to greet him. Luis must have been tired; all the same he took the time to stop at every house, asking after each neighbor's health, wishing each one good fortune.

Luis looked like a man now, an important man of the church, no longer a boy. Coming toward us, he was almost a stranger; he wore the black coat with the red sash of a seminary student. Then Luis jumped up and down and waved and at last he looked like himself, my dear brother. A boy with long legs and the dark raven eyes that were our heritage, who carried a huge weight on his shoulders: the great man he was to be someday.

I ran up to him and hugged him.

Raven, he said, using my childhood name, *I wish you could fly to visit me. Not that I miss you.* He grinned.

Not that I miss you either, I teased back. I hugged him tighter. I missed him so much I could feel it at every hour of the day.

You look grown up, my brother said.

When our grandmother is done with you, you'll look fattened up, I teased.

In Luis's honor, my grandmother was making a special dinner: *burkas,* grape leaves filled with feta cheese, and kabobs flavored with cinnamon and garlic. My grandfather had put on his fancy black suit; at last, he looked happy. Luis was everything to him. My brother had been gone a year, and we all wished he had more than a few days to spend with us. His studies were important, and he wanted to get back and finish as quickly as possible. Luis was a dedicated student; he had a habit of closing his eyes when he said the rosary. He could read Greek, Latin, Spanish, Hebrew, Arabic. He could speak with my grandfather in a special language — called *Ladino* — a mix of two languages, Hebrew and Spanish.

My mother put rouge on her cheeks and pulled her hair up with combs made of shells; she wore her finest dress and a silk shawl made in Istanbul. From the moment my brother arrived, Abra barely let him out of her sight. There was so little time for Luis to be with us that we all wanted his attention.

The priest from our church, Friar deLeon, who had recommended Luis to the seminary, came to our house for dinner. On Sundays we always went to his church, even though it was on the other side of town, and Our Lady of Mercy was right down the street from our house. We preferred the Chapel of All Saints; most of our friends did, and my grandfather said it was best to worship with those you knew well. When Luis was finished with his studies, he would come back to our church. He would be one of the most important men in town, on every committee, even sitting on the mayor's council.

Friar deLeon watched as my grandmother lit the candles. It wasn't yet completely dark, but it was our way to light the candles in our silver candlesticks before we began our Friday dinner.

We give thanks to our Lord, Friar deLeon said.

It was an honor to have the priest in our home. Everyone murmured, *Amen.* Members of our church crossed ourselves in a special way. Head, lips, shoulder, shoulder. I whispered to Luis that when I ate dinner at Catalina's house, they crossed themselves in a different way.

We do it this way so God knows what's in our hearts, Luis explained to me when I asked about it now. He looked at me strangely, perhaps to see if I would say something back to him.

Let's go on with dinner, my grandfather said to Luis, and immediately Luis stopped explaining things to me. Luis served the adafina I had made, our Friday night chicken stew. I had added some of the basil I had grown in my brother's honor. That herb brought good luck and long life, or so I'd heard. For the first time, everyone declared the dish delicious. Even my grandmother didn't tell me what I'd done wrong.

For me, that was lucky indeed.

I MOVED OUT of my chamber, where Luis used to sleep, so he could reclaim the room. I went back to a mat on the floor beside my mother's bed. I didn't mind. Luis made you want to give things up for him, he was so generous and so good. He had brought gifts for everyone, even the little Arrias girls next door. In his bag there was lavender water, candied figs, a special book for my grandfather. For me, my brother had brought a tin of rouge made out of a flower from a faraway land that was the same color as the red lily that grew in the Muslim doctor's wife's garden.

My brother was tired, and he slept during most of his time with us. At the seminary, Luis had to study all day and all night. He copied manuscripts for the Bishop, and his fingers were stained with ink. Here at home, he went to the Friar's chapel in the afternoons, and studied, but in the evenings, after dinner, he let my mother use his strong arms so she could wind her yarn into even lengths around them. He laughed and told jokes, although when he slept he spoke Latin and Greek, as if he were still studying in his dreams.

Catalina knocked on our door the day after my brother arrived home, but my grandmother shooed her back home; she told Catalina we were too busy to have any visitors. Luis needed peace and quiet; he needed his rest. Later, when Catalina came back, Luis was reading in the yard, and he didn't even look up from his book. He thought a hired girl had come to work in the fields, and he'd told her to come back another time, when he wasn't studying.

Your brother thinks he's so special and important, Catalina said later when we met at the well in the Plaza. I had gone back and forth to the well three times that day so my grandmother could wash all of my brother's clothes. *He doesn't seem so special to me.*

My brother was too busy with his studies to notice things that were obvious to other people. He forgot the dinner hour. He forgot to wash his face. Even when he lived with us, he was more often at the church than he was home.

Well, he is special, I said. *He doesn't have time for foolish things.*

Really? There was something in Catalina's voice I hadn't heard before. *Are you saying I'm a fool?*

I felt my heart sink. She was angry. I hadn't meant for that.

I'm only saying that you and I don't have to study like Luis. We're lucky. We can do as we please.

Your brother is just like everybody else, you know, Catalina said as we walked home. *No better. And maybe worse. I hate people who think they're better than everyone else.*

I thought of saying something, but I didn't. All of our lives, I had told Catalina everything. Now I was afraid not just of what I might say, but of what she might hear. She didn't seem like the Catalina I had always known.

We walked along together, the water sloshing out of our buckets. Well water, cold water, water that was so heavy it was difficult to balance the buckets.

Look, there's a dove, I said, pointing to the fields beyond our houses.

A dove in the garden was good luck, a sign of excellent crops to come.

Don't be silly. We had reached Catalina's yard. *It's a hawk.* She seemed pleased by my mistake.

CATALINA SAID I should ask my mother if I could come to her house for dinner. Her mother was making sausage, the hot kind. Didn't I just love those? I was surprised that Catalina didn't remember I never ate sausage.

I told Catalina I was having my stomach sickness. Another lie. I suppose in some way what I said was the truth. I wasn't avoiding dinner at Catalina's because of the sausage that I could push to the side of my plate, or because Luis had so few nights at home before he had to return to the seminary. It was Catalina. She was the reason my stomach hurt. I wasn't quite as certain that I knew her down to her soul.

When it came right down to it, I wasn't so sure she knew me either.

My brother was the sort of person who could tell how other people felt just by looking at them. He knew that I missed him. He made time for me alone. That evening instead of going to Catalina's house, my brother and I went walking up into the hills to look for lavender to bring home to my mother, which was her cure for headaches and fevers.

Luis let me take my little pig along; we fashioned

a collar out of yarn and led Dini with a rope. We laughed when the pig found some mushrooms right away and when he wouldn't move after we came upon a berry bush. We had to stand there each time and let Dini eat his fill; when he still wouldn't budge, my brother picked up the pig and carried him. We laughed together till our sides hurt.

Your baby is too fat, my brother teased me.

I felt we had stepped back in time, before Luis had become so serious. Even now Luis seemed too young to be a priest. I wanted him to stay at home, to be my brother again and not someone who soon would be an important man. Some people like Catalina might resent his high position.

Are you sure the seminary is what you want? I asked my brother.

Luis was holding bunches of lavender. He was kind and thoughtful; some girl would have been so lucky to have him as her husband.

I want to protect and serve our people, Luis said.

We walked back in silence.

My brother's answer had not meant yes. It had meant our grandfather wanted this future for my brother, and as a loyal grandson, Luis's life was in our grandfather's hands. Like Friar deLeon, Luis would soon be privy to the town government's decisions and the church's edicts. A priest gained favors and gave them, and our family and friends would do well because of this. I wondered if Luis would always be leaving us, if even when he was walking beside me he would be somewhere else, divided between place and time, between the *now* and the *soon to be.* I wondered if I would always think about the life he might have had, with a family of his own, a future of his own choosing.

ON THE DAY Luis left, I went out to the fields. I wanted to be alone. Now I saw that Catalina had indeed been right. It was a hawk that flew above the crops. The hawk had made a home in one of the olive trees, and the songbirds were too fearful to fly across the sky, except in the earliest morning hours, when the hawk was still out in the hills, hunting. I called to the hawk. I brought crusts of bread and orange slices, but it ignored me.

The next day I climbed up into the olive tree and talked to the hawk. I stayed up in the branches for nearly an hour, but it did no good. I couldn't make a pet out of such a creature. I couldn't even get the hawk to listen to me.

I saw Andres in the place where he'd been digging the irrigation trough for his uncle. He had been watching me while I perched in the tree. I sat there a while longer. If Andres came over to me, then it was meant to be, and if he didn't, then it would be just like the hawk. There would be nothing I could do about it if he approached. I wouldn't be to blame, even though he was promised to Catalina. You can't tame something that doesn't wish to be tamed, any more than you can make someone love you. All you can do is wait and see what will happen.

Andres walked over when the clouds turned a deep blue, the color of lakes, a color that can chill you even on a hot summer day.

You're not meaning to fly away from me, are you? Andres said as he approached.

I mistook a hawk for a dove, I said.

Andres helped me down from the tree.

I smelled like olives and tree bark; my hands were dirty, but I didn't care, and neither, it seemed, did he.

It's a common mistake, Andres said.

It wasn't and I knew it, but I smiled at him anyway.

The distance I felt from Catalina was like a rock inside of me. I thought I would feel lighter if I told someone the truth.

I can't tell Catalina about the way I feel about some things anymore, I told Andres.

Neither can I, Andres said. We were both looking up at the sky. I suppose we were making too much noise for the hawk; it left its perch in the olive tree. The songbirds began calling to one another now. *But I can talk to you,* he told me.

After that we just stood there silently, with nothing needing to be said. I did feel lighter; I was aware of the air all around me and of the heat of the day and of how close Andres was.

Even though I was standing on the ground, I had to hold onto the olive tree for fear I might fall.

———— • ◆ • ————

THAT NIGHT in bed, I had the feeling that my world was moving too fast. Was this how the hawk saw our world from the reaches of the sky? Everything was a blur; the days we were living in were disappearing much too quickly.

I had my own chamber again now that Luis was gone, but I didn't want to be there. I went to my mother's room and slept on a rug beside her bed. I looked out her window to watch the stars in the sky. Was I wrong to fall in love with Andres? Was it destiny or just a betrayal?

My mother didn't wake; she was dreaming, I was sure of it. I hoped she would dream something for me. A gate that led to a garden, a dove that came when I called to it, time enough to live out my life side by side with the one I loved.

ANGELS

Never Trust

Stone

The day when the arrests began reminded me of the day of the burning books, when the air was filled with sparks, when something bad crept out onto the Plaza from the deep, evil place, something that would become so strong no one could catch it or beat it down or lock it away.

Now I understand those days were not really a beginning but a continuation. A monster is hard to see and even harder to kill. It takes time to grow so huge, time to crawl up into the open air. People will tell you it's not there; you're imagining things. But a book is a book. Pages are pages. Hawks are hawks. Doves are doves.

Hatred is always hatred.

———— ◦ ◆ ◦ ————

THE ARRIAS FAMILY who lived in the house beside ours were all arrested early in the morning. The mother, Miriam, was screaming when they took her; the father, Juan, was beaten down by soldiers and dragged away. Soldiers also took the two children, Marianna and Antonia, little girls who couldn't have hurt anyone.

My grandmother told me not to leave the house. We watched from the window. It was horrible when Señora Arrias tried to get to her children, but as soon as I pushed against the door to go to help her, my grandmother grabbed me.

Stay, she said to me.

When I pulled away, my mother cried out, *This time you'll do what your grandmother tells you to do!*

The tone of my mother's voice made me obey. I had never heard her sound this way.

What did the Arriases do? I asked. *They would never commit a crime.*

My grandmother laughed. It was a terrible sound. It sounded as though she might cry. Something my grandmother never did.

They were Conversos, *New Christians. Their families converted a hundred years ago when the Jews were being expelled from our country. Now they've been accused of practicing their religion, of being* Marranos.

I looked at my grandmother, confused. The Arriases were good friends of our family. The children were sweet girls who liked to play with our chickens and collect feathers to make necklaces for their mother. We could hear Marianna screaming for her mother now.

A Marrano *is a secret Jew,* my grandmother told me.

But they go to our church, I said.

That's right, my grandmother said. *For all the good it did them.*

What will the soldiers do? I wanted to know.

You know what Marrano means? My grandmother was really looking at me, really talking to me; I was even more afraid of her than usual. *It means pig. What do you think they'll do to people they consider to be pigs? They'll cook them, God help us. They'll burn them alive.*

Stop talking! My grandfather said in a terrifying voice. Now I knew why his students appeared so humble before him. He scared me so much I was shaking. *Don't tell this girl any more!*

THERE WAS BLOOD on the path between the Arriases' house and ours; but when my grandmother wanted to wash it away, my grandfather stopped her.

Let everyone see the blood, he said. *Don't clean it up. That's the only way people remember.*

I went out to the garden and was sick to my stomach. I got some water from the rain barrel and washed away not only my sickness but also the blood on the path. I did what I could, but my grandfather had been right; it was useless. The blood had stained the bricks and wouldn't wash away.

I went back to our yard and sat on the steps. I didn't care that the chickens were clucking and pecking at my shoes. My dear Dini came running to me. He made sad noises and lay down beside me. He was a comfort, even in this time. I would never let anyone cook him. It was such a horrible thought, I erased it from my mind.

I walked over to the Arrias house and I saw that my mother had told me the truth; tears did have a color. Where Marianna and Antonia Arrias had stood crying for their mother, there was a blue stain on the stones. I picked up one of the stones, and it was cool in the palm of my hand. When I held it to my ear, I could hear the sound of the little girls. The stone was weeping.

I threw it away, into the thornbushes, where the tall grass grew. I didn't need to listen to a stone to hear what had happened. I didn't need to see blood on the bricks. I could hear the crying inside my head; I could see the blood inside my head. It was with me forever, whether or not I wanted to forget.

EVERYONE was talking about the Arriases' trial. The rumors were terrible. There were whispers on the street and in the Plaza, slander spoken as though it were pure and true. Some said that Señora Arrias killed small children, and that was the reason her sunflowers grew so well, because she sprinkled the children's blood on the ground.

Others swore the Señor practiced magic that ruined his neighbors' crops. Together, they had taught their daughters the devil's language. They had made the rainy season last so long that there were many bad olives on the trees.

On one thing everyone seemed to agree: The Arriases were Jews who were only pretending to be Christian. Someone had turned them in, and although the witness was never named in court, his testimony was believed by the judge. Once a person was officially accused, there was no argument and no defense. The accusation itself sealed a person's guilt.

The judge had come from a hundred miles away; he was living in the old Duke's palace. The armory behind the palace was also populated now; it had been turned into a prison. If anyone was arrested, they were sent to the armory; their children were given away to an old, respected Christian family who would raise them properly. As for the accused, a conviction of heresy meant one thing: death.

Our family prayed for the Arriases; our whole congregation did. Friar deLeon said a special prayer for them, one I had never heard before, a plea to St. Esther, a saint he said was invoked only at the most terrible of times. She was a queen who had to pretend she was someone other than her truest self in order to save her people. She was so beautiful, my grandmother whispered as we sat in the cool, dark church, that the persecutors who wanted to hurt her people believed whatever she told them.

Some lies were to hurt and some were to heal, my grandmother told me. I wasn't so sure. I hadn't wanted to hurt Catalina, so I didn't tell her about the way I felt about Andres. But now there was a distance between us.

Just because something is unspoken doesn't mean that it disappears.

That evening, before dinner, while I was still wearing my Sunday clothes and the strand of pearls my grandparents had bought for me on the day I was born, I saw something through the window. There was a shadow inside the Arriases' house. I knew I shouldn't go next door, but I did. Maybe it was a bad spirit or a curse brought to life. But it could be something else. Perhaps

Marianna had run away from the new family she'd been given to and was hiding in her old house. Perhaps the arrest had been recognized as a terrible mistake and the officials had let the family go. Could it be that they were back living their lives in their own house, free from terror?

But it was nothing like that. Nothing at all. I crouched by the window so I wouldn't be seen. When I peered over the ledge I could see Catalina and her mother going through the drawers on the tall wooden bureau, taking out the linens Señora Arrias had stitched. Señora Arrias made beautiful lace, intricate as a map of the stars.

Catalina and her mother forced open another drawer and then rejoiced; there was the silverware, the candlesticks the family used on Friday nights.

I ran back to my house, breathless, my legs shaking.

That very evening Catalina and I were supposed to have a needlepoint lesson from her mother. The thought of it made me sick. Just as I'd heard that blue stone weeping, I saw Catalina grabbing the silver when I closed my eyes. Some things you cannot wish away or think away. They become a part of you when you remember them.

I thought over what I would do, as though Catalina were no longer my friend, but someone I had to trick. When the heat of the day was over, I went to Catalina's house at the time of our lesson and knocked on the door. I knew Andres was there and that he'd be waiting for a good excuse to join us—he'd bring us some fruit perhaps, or cold water; all the while he'd be trying to send me a message in the way he looked at me, and I would try not to let anyone see when I sent him a message back.

Usually I would be happy about such plans, but when Catalina opened the door I told her I had to miss our needlepoint lesson.

I was sick today, I told her. It didn't even feel like a lie. *I keep having pains in my stomach.*

But we planned this! My mother has been expecting you!

I couldn't help but wonder if Catalina's mother had something to do with the Arriases' arrest. Certainly, she had been quick to denounce them in public after the trial. She'd been quick to take what belonged to them.

I wouldn't want to bring up my dinner in your house, I said. I knew Catalina was squeamish—and indeed, she backed away.

Promise me we'll do it tomorrow, Catalina said.

She made me curl my little finger with hers to seal the bargain, and then she had us both make the sign of the cross. I hoped God wasn't judging me too harshly for not confronting Catalina about being in the Arriases' house. I made the sign of the cross the way my family always did: forehead, lips, shoulders.

Everyone in your family does that all wrong, Catalina said.

No, we don't, I said.

I was thinking about how we went to the same church as the Arrias family. I was thinking about the look on my grandmother's face when they were arrested.

When I went to leave, Catalina stopped me.

Let me wear your pearls to seal the promise.

I reached up and touched the necklace at my throat. It was the only thing of value that I owned. The only gift my grandparents had ever given me. Catalina saw me hesitate.

Maybe you're not as good a friend as I thought you were, she said.

Why would you think that?

Catalina shrugged. *It seems I can't depend on you for anything.*

Then she backed off; her pride had been hurt. She wasn't certain she wanted anything from me now. And what did I want?

For everything to be the same as it had been.

For Catalina to be my friend once again.

You can depend on me, I said. I wanted it to be true, as it had been in the past. *Take them,* I said. *I want you to have them.*

I took off the pearls and watched as my friend fastened them around her neck. Wearing them, she looked exactly the same, my oldest, dearest friend, Catalina.

How do I look? she asked.

I had never noticed how much the outside of things mattered to Catalina.

Beautiful, I said.

That was enough for her. That was what she wanted.

But what I really meant was: *They are still mine.*

That was my third lie to Catalina.

After three there was no point in counting.

SOON ENOUGH, another decree went up in the Plaza, posted directly across from the well of heaven. Citizens were to report anyone they suspected of being false Christians to the court. If they did not, they themselves might be found guilty of heresy, jailed, and then judged.

The Plaza was crowded and noisy. There were many strangers in town, from cities that were far away. Vendors with carts were selling filled grape leaves and almond cakes the way they did at festivals. There was a juggler who threw silk scarves into the air and caught them as they fell back to earth. There was a man selling rabbits, skinned and bloody, their bodies hanging from a pole he wore across his back.

The area around the decree was so mobbed, I had to read it from a distance, squinting my eyes, concentrating hard in order to make out the letters. At last I could see.

There was a list of the ways to tell who was a hidden Jew:

They wear clean clothes on Saturday.

We did that, but only to air out our best clothes to wear to Sunday Mass.

They light candles on Friday night.

We did that, but only to see by candlelight, for soon enough it would be dark.

They fast twice a year.

We did that, but only to remember my father.

They tell stories of Queen Esther.

We did that, but only because she was a saint spoken about in church.

They do not eat pork.

We did that, but simply because we preferred vegetables and fresh green things.

They name their children after those in the Old Testament.

We did that, but they were only our pet names that meant nothing to anyone but each other. The name of love my grandfather called my grandmother that sounded like knives—Sarah. The name my mother used to call me when I was small as she rocked me to sleep that was also the name my grandmother called me when she gave me the strand of pearls.

Esther.

Turn one in, and you share all he owns, halved with the court.

People were looking at each other with their eyes cast down, only daring to sneak looks at one another; with a single decree the world was viewed differently, filled with dangerous possibilities. I felt as I had on that first burning day when there were cinders in my hair. Standing there, surrounded by my neighbors, in a village where my family had lived for five hundred years, I could think of only one thing:

We did that.

INSTEAD OF going home, I went into the hills where my mother and I so often went to search for herbs. I walked fast so I couldn't think. I wanted it that way. Otherwise I would think about Catalina and her mother rummaging through the Arriases' house. I would wonder if my name were really Esther.

I went deep into the woods, where there were pine trees and a carpet of soft needles that made everything quiet. But I didn't want quiet. I didn't want to know any secrets. Why we went to the same church as the Arrias family. Why we had special names. I wanted to be who I'd always been. Was that too much to ask?

I started to run. I ran until my ears were pounding. Until I couldn't take another breath. I thought I'd been running aimlessly, without a thought in my head. But I had been following a map I didn't know I kept inside my heart. Soon enough, I found myself in the grove where my father was buried. I had remembered.

I hadn't been here in a very long time. Not since I was a little girl. But I must have recalled there were pine trees. I must have remembered the way deep inside.

There was a flat blue stone to mark his grave, and on that stone, engraved too deeply ever to disappear, was a star. I thought of my name. Estrella. My father's dark star. I thought about all the secrets in my house. I thought about the way we loved each other. When I was a little girl and came here with my mother, we had left two small stones on my father's gravestone to mark our remembrance. I did that now.

It took me a long time to return to the hill overlooking our town. When I got there and looked down, there was nothing I felt I wanted from that place. Usually I felt I was gazing at my home; now it was only a cluster of houses, tile roofs, fields and meadows, and trees. It might have been anyplace, somewhere I'd never been before.

Love

In the outskirts, the Muslim quarter was quiet, but the closer I got to the center of the village, the noisier it became. There were riots in the Plaza, neighbor turned against neighbor. Bloody betrayal on every step. Shops had their locks and doors ripped away. People were carrying stolen goods on their backs: rugs and kettles and bolts of cloth. It might have seemed like a carnival except for the screaming, and the rising smoke, and the bitterness in the air. The lime trees in the Plaza had been set on fire. Lime trees when they burn smell black and evil, like honey when it's scalded, like rotten fruit. People said those trees had always been there and that our town would continue as long as they flowered and grew.

Andres had been waiting for me at the edge of our neighborhood. He'd seen me run off and had been worried.

This is no time to be wandering around, he said.

I have the feeling I don't even know who I am.

It was the time when anything could happen. It was the time when a single word could turn your world upside down.

Don't worry. I know who you are in your heart, Andres said. *That's all that matters.*

And that was it. That was the moment. Now I knew how I would feel if I ever lost him. That was how you knew love. My mother had told me that. All you had to do was imagine your life without the other person, and if the thought alone made you shiver, then you knew.

Andres walked me home in silence; we stayed as near to one another as we dared. It had never taken that long to walk home before, and all the while I wished it would last an eternity. He kissed me when we reached the gate of my house. It was dark and no one could see; all the same I felt as though I were burning so brightly everyone in every house could see the light inside of me.

That was how I knew what the gate in my dreams was made of. It was made of this.

I WENT TO SPEAK to my grandmother. I was afraid to ask her the questions I needed to have answered, so I said the rosary before I had the courage to approach her. She was kneading dough at the big table. Our table was so old you could see the dents in the wood where my great-great-grandmother had chopped vegetables. My great-great-grandmother had kneaded bread here so often, the table curved down in the center, and now my grandmother was kneading bread in the very same place. She added olives and garlic to the mix, then braided the dough in three parts so that it rose prettily. My grandmother's way of dealing with the riots in the Plaza was not to go there and not to think about it.

But I had been there. I'd read the decree.

My grandmother was not the sort of person you could fool with pretty words and long, drawn-out requests.

I have questions for you, I said.

I'm too busy. She didn't even look at me.

Am I Esther?

My grandmother stopped kneading the dough for the briefest instant, then she continued. No answer, so I tried another question.

Are you Sarah? I asked.

Now my grandmother stopped her work. She pushed the dough away and looked at me. She had never looked at me in this way. She had been too busy hiding things from me. For an instant I could see inside of her. She had stopped protecting me from the truth, and it glimmered between us.

So it was true. I felt my face grow hot. Was everything I'd ever thought and said and done been a lie?

And no one ever told me?

Once you know some things, you can't unknow them. It's a burden that can never be given away.

I felt so hot and so stupid; I ran to my chamber and threw myself on my bed. My pallet was made of fresh straw, but I was like the lime now and not the flower. Bitterness longs for bitterness.

My grandmother came after me and sat on the edge of the bed.

We planned to tell you, she said.

When? When I was in my grave?

I'm telling you now. We are Jews and we always have been, but the only way for us to survive is to pretend to be something else.

I sat up, my face burning with tears. Maybe they were clear or maybe they were blue. What difference did it make?

Marranos, I said. *Pigs.*

My grandmother looked as though she wanted to slap me, but she didn't. It was the truth after all. That's what they called us.

You have to tell Luis, I said. *He's living a lie. He'll be furious.*

Luis knows. He will take over from Friar deLeon someday so he can protect our people, just as the Friar has. This is how we have a voice the town fathers will listen to.

You told Luis but not me! Because I'm nothing to you!

The world had indeed changed if this was the way I was speaking to my grandmother.

Exactly the opposite, my grandmother said. *We kept silent because we didn't want you to carry the burden before you had to.*

When I was a little girl, I had wished my grandmother would come and tell me a story at night, but she barely glanced at me when I went off to bed. Now I refused to look at her.

This kind of knowing you can never tell to anyone. If you want us to survive, you cannot trust a soul.

My grandmother ran her hands over my hair.

Esther, she said.

It was my name after all. My secret name. The one I could never use.

I looked up at my grandmother.

For the first time in my life, I wasn't afraid of her.

LATE THAT NIGHT, my mother woke me. She shook me, then signaled for me to follow. The moon had risen, and everything looked white. I pulled my cloak on over my nightclothes and stepped into my shoes.

I felt I must be dreaming, but the road we were walking on was very real. We didn't speak as we made our way through town. Still, I knew my grandmother and my mother had talked about me. Now it seemed they had decided they would trust me with their knowledge. My mother reminded me I could tell no one where she was taking me.

Not for any reason on this earth. You can never tell, my mother told me.

I swore I would not.

I did not tell her that when she woke me, I had been standing in a garden in my dreams. Someone had called me *Esther.*

Esther, the voice had said in my dream. *Those you love will not drown or burn. They will fly away.*

My mother was so at home in the woods she didn't notice when her skirts caught on thorns; little blue flags were left behind. I had to struggle to keep up with her. My breathing was so hard my sides hurt; still we went on. There were stones, but we went around them. There were low branches, but we ducked beneath them. There was a small stream, but we found our way over by stepping on some flat rocks.

We passed hidden graves on the way, all with blue stone markers, each engraved with a star. We didn't stop until we came to a far place, one that was even more distant than the spot where my father was buried. We walked through a grove of plum trees, then crawled through a tall hedge covered by white blooming flowers. In the clearing on the other side of the hedge there was a pool made from cedar wood planks. My mother said the pool was very old and had to be repaired and filled with clean rainwater once a year by the men of our church. My mother told me the word for this wooden rainwater holder was called a *mikva,* a bath. It was only for women, to purify us and make us stronger. All of the women in our church shared our secret; all journeyed here when they came of age.

My mother pinned up her long hair and took off her clothes. She was so beautiful, I was stunned. I felt like nothing compared to her, a child; but when she told me to undress and enter the bath with her, I did.

We floated in the dark water. Above us the sky was so filled with stars, it seemed more white than black. I thought of salt and flour on my grandmother's tabletop. I thought of pearls in the sea. All this way from town we could still breathe in the odor of the lime flowers from the burnt trees in the Plaza. Some things were strong; they stayed with you. The place where you grew up, the scent of lime flowers, the dreams you had. When I stared into the bathwater, I thought of the bowl of water my mother had me gaze into so many times, and I thought, *It is all here. The beginning and the end.*

Later, when I dressed, I could feel the burden of who we were. All the same, I felt like my truest self walking under the stars, so clean I shivered, so much who I was and always had been, whether or not they'd told me.

It was a long way back to town, and I had one more question to ask.

Why didn't our great-great-grandparents leave this place instead of living false lives?

The court took the children when they cast out the Jews. They wouldn't give them back until the people of your great-great-grandparents' time converted.

They should have run away after that.

We've always lived here, my mother said. *Five hundred years of bones are in this earth.*

My mother knew how hard it was to leave the dead. But didn't we carry them with us? Wasn't my father with us as long as we thought of him?

We walked the rest of the way in silence. It was nearly sunrise when we sneaked into our own yard, our own house. We stopped in the yard and took off our shoes so we wouldn't wake my grandfather. The chickens were still asleep, but there was the hawk above the fields, making its way through the lightening sky. I had seen these same fields every day of my life, the same olive and almond trees, the same horizon. Still, I couldn't help but wonder if it was a mistake for people like us to be tied to a place. If we weren't meant to be ready and willing to wander. If everything we needed was contained in who we were.

And what we remembered.

DARKENING

LIGHT

Who Can You Tell

Sorrow

Over the next few days, there was so much looting that the streets became too dangerous to walk. My grandfather made a new lock for our door and nailed the windows shut. We did not go to the market or the dye vats or to the well in the Plaza. We took in the animals at night, letting the chickens lay their eggs on our rugs, the sheep shelter under our table, allowing the pigs to sleep beside the stove, all except for Dini, whom I sneaked up to my room at night.

Dini was very well behaved and quiet; he slept on a pile of rags, curled up in a corner. I could hear him snuffling in his dreams while I fell asleep, happy enough just to be near me. I wished I could sleep as deeply as he did. I wished I could be so easily comforted.

ONE EVENING, I went out for walk with Catalina. We were both restless, and we missed each other. Maybe I was wrong about the distance between us. Maybe we could be friends. Crow and Raven. Two girls who looked like sisters, with the same long black hair. Two girls who believed they could be anything they wanted to be.

Remember when we used to pretend we were donkeys and run through the field? I asked.

We were silly children, Catalina said.

You were faster than I was, I said.

I was. Catalina looked pleased.

In truth, I always slowed down at the end of every race. I was the sort of donkey who didn't need to win. Maybe that was why whenever Catalina wanted something of mine, I was only too happy to give it to her.

But you were prettier, Catalina said.

She had slipped her arm away from mine.

A donkey is a donkey. I laughed. *None are pretty.*

That may be, Catalina said, *but some birds are called ravens and others are called crows. We're too old to pretend anymore.* Catalina stopped and gave me a hard stare. *I don't like the way you look at Andres,* she said.

I wanted to say *I can't help myself,* but I didn't say anything.

Stay away from him, Catalina said. *I won't tell you again.*

ONE MORNING when we woke up, we found that a window had been pried open. Someone had broken in. My grandmother checked and made sure that her greatest treasure, her silver candlesticks, were still there. She searched through the rest of our belongings. All the robbers seemed to have taken was food. Olives, flour, a jar of honey. People were afraid to go to the shops or even to work in their own fields. These days it was not safe for a woman to venture to the market alone, lest she be taken by soldiers and questioned about her friends and neighbors. My grandmother decided that from that day forward she would leave a basket of food in the yard for anyone who might be hungry.

After we'd set out some bread and feta cheese for passersby, my grandmother turned to me and asked where my pearls were. Could they have been stolen?

I'm sure they're here, I said.

I went to my room and pretended to search for them, then returned and told my grandmother I had found my necklace, stored in a box where I kept trinkets.

You should have put them on, my grandmother said. *They would be safe around your neck.*

I said that the weather had been so hot I couldn't bear the feel of anything against my skin.

My grandmother narrowed her eyes.

Pearls come from the sea. They're always cool.

My grandmother wasn't an easy person to lie to. Still, I had begun; as terrible as it felt, I had to carry on.

I'll wear them to dinner, I told my grandmother.

I went to Catalina's house right away, even though I dreaded seeing her. I couldn't believe I'd given something so precious away.

I knocked again and again, but no one responded. I thought I heard voices from inside the house.

Finally I called out Catalina's name. It took a long time for her to come to see who was there.

So a raven comes calling on a crow, she said.

I need the pearls back, I told her. *My grandmother asked me where they were.*

You gave them to me, Catalina said.

Catalina stood behind the opened door. There were little black flies in the air, so tiny it wasn't possible to see them; all the same, they bit. Even the chickens in Catalina's yard were seeking refuge under the house.

I know, I said, *but now I need them.*

You made me take them. You told me to!

I looked into Catalina's eyes. I had known her so long, my whole life, and I'd never noticed they were green.

I need them back, I told her, hoping my voice would sound stronger than I was.

There was a pause, and then Catalina said, *I need them more.*

Andres must have heard us talking. He came outside and called my name joyfully. He said the word *Estrella* as though it meant *beautiful,* and *you belong to me,* and *shining star.*

I saw the look on Catalina's face. Maybe I deserved it. Maybe I was at fault.

Estrella is leaving, Catalina said to Andres.

I need the necklace, I told Catalina.

The way she looked at me was with the face of a different Catalina than the one I had known. Something inside me started pounding, as though I had a dove trapped inside my chest.

Well, it's not yours anymore.

Catalina went inside and slammed the door.

Andres and I stood there.

Why is she so angry? he asked.

I told him about the pearls, even though I knew it was something more. Catalina was mad that I was me and she was herself. She was mad that Andres was standing here talking to me; that he'd said my name as though it were a secret we shared.

There was nothing I could do about Catalina. I thought my grandmother might have been right in what she once told me.

You think you know somebody, but what do you know? Only what they want to show you. Remember, it's what's inside that matters.

Catalina called from the house for Andres to come in for dinner.

Wait here, he told me.

Andres went in, and when he returned he had my pearls. I put out my hand, but instead he looped the pearls around my throat and fastened them. Andres walked me home. My heart was beating against my chest so hard it was as if someone were throwing stones at me. I felt that anything could happen. Anything at all.

Andres did not look happy, and he did not walk close to me. Finally, I asked what was wrong.

When I went inside to get your pearls, Catalina told me you're in love with someone, Andres said.

Maybe I am.

She said it was someone named Philippe who works at the dye vats. She said you wanted the pearls back so badly because he gave them to you.

My grandparents gave me these pearls. And that boy she's talking about—I don't even know him. He's not the one. I said it so Andres would know the truth.

Andres took my hand, and I let him. I tried to think about water in a bowl, about a river that is always moving and changing, about a garden that had ten gates, but all I could think of was him. We kissed beside the fence, in a way that left me dizzy. We laughed at the way we felt. At how dizzy we both were. We kissed again to make sure that the way we felt inside was real, and it was.

Don't let your grandfather promise you to anyone, Andres said.

My grandfather doesn't make my choices.

It was a cool night, but I was burning. I felt the way I did when my mother taught me the whirling dance, the one only men are supposed to do, the mystic dance that makes the garden bright inside your head.

Andres laughed. *Then don't promise yourself to anyone. Just to me. We don't have to tell if you don't want to. It will be a promise for us alone to share.*

How could I make a promise when I knew how Catalina felt about Andres? Still, how could I give him up?

What about Catalina? I finally asked. *I thought you were going to marry her.*

That was never going to happen. Not with her.

I REMEMBERED what my mother had told me about the first time she saw my father. How when he turned around to look at her, she felt she'd been slapped. How she tried stop the way she felt about him; how she pretended she didn't care until she made herself sick to her stomach. Once she had seen him, it was as though she had swallowed a thousand knives. She tried not to feel it, but every time she saw him, there was that knife.

I could feel it now stabbing me in the center of my chest. Maybe it was love or maybe I was pierced by the look on Catalina's face as she watched us from her yard. She'd come back outside after Andres had left with me and she was still there, staring. She'd been watching all along. I wished she hadn't seen us. I wished we were strangers. I wished I had met Andres hundreds of miles away from Encaleflora.

No wonder Catalina's feelings about me had turned into dark, night thoughts. Catalina had no idea of who I was. I was Esther, in love with her cousin and never once saying a word about it. Esther, the girl with a secret life. Esther, who had seen Catalina stealing silver and linen.

I told Andres I could not promise myself to him so easily.

I told him that because it was less difficult than telling him the truth.

I wasn't certain I deserved him.

THAT NIGHT I couldn't eat my dinner, and later I couldn't sleep. I wondered how Andres would react if he knew I was a hidden Jew, not a Christian as he was. By law we could not marry; we could not even talk or share a meal; if we dared to do so, it was heresy, the worst offense imaginable.

I unclasped the pearls and put them in my trinket box, where I kept little treasures, mostly things Catalina and I had collected when we went into the hills. There were blue bird feathers, pressed flowers, a note Catalina had written me on my last birthday with a silly poem that said we were like two trees growing in the same garden. I put the treasure box under the pallet on my bed. I slept on it. At first it was lumpy and I was too aware of it to sleep well. But after a few nights,

I didn't feel it at all, and by the next week, I forgot anything was there.

THE RIOTS on the Plaza had quieted down; people came and went again, to the fields, to market, to the well where the water came directly from heaven. Still, in my house we were uneasy. One day my mother spread her cards out on a table to see what our future might hold. Right away, she made a face. She didn't like what she saw before us.

It's a bad time to be in the world, she said.

My mother tied a piece of red yarn around my arm, under my clothing, for luck, she said. It was a secret amulet. She then tied the red thread around her own arm as well.

She reshuffled the cards again and laid them out once more. The letters were all the same.

Something's about to happen, my mother told me.

I didn't like how upset she seemed, so I tried to make light of what the cards told her.

Something's always about to happen, I said.

This will be different. It will start with one sorrow

and then build into a thousand. There will be so many
sorrows, they will be like the stars in the sky.

I KEPT LOOKING for an omen. But our lives went
on as usual; the world began to feel normal
again—no burnings, no arrests, just summer afternoons and deep blue evenings.

And then, one bright day, I heard a nightingale
in the fields. It was noontime, not the hour for
such things. My mother had told me that birds
and animals know the future before we do. They
try to warn us, but we just don't listen.

I ran outside to try to chase the nightingale
away, but I couldn't spy it. It just kept singing a
mourning song.

My mother came outside and stood behind me.
She placed a hand on my shoulder.

Now we begin, she said.

SOON ENOUGH, a Muslim boy appeared in
our yard.

Other than my mother, most people from our

neighborhood would not go to the Muslim quarter. Perhaps some might venture to the shops, or, if they were very ill, they might visit the doctor. As for the Muslims, they did not come to our part of town.

But there was the boy in our yard. He was the one we had seen doing yard work at the doctor's house. The boy looked nervous; he held two very large wooden boxes. I wondered if they were treasure boxes; I wondered if this was a good omen that might prove my mother's cards wrong.

When my grandmother spied the boy, she hurried into the yard yelling, trying to chase him away. The boy stood his ground and yelled back at her in Arabic and Spanish, but neither understood the other. My mother came running out of the house. She shushed my grandmother—something she never did—and she listened to the boy. My mother's hair was loose, and her feet were bare, and the boy looked surprised. Out of respect, he looked down at the dirt when he spoke. I could now hear there were chickens clucking like mad inside the boxes.

Our own dusty chickens had scattered to hide under the house, where it was cool and protected.

When my mother nodded, the boy set down the boxes and ran out of our yard. It wasn't safe for him to be in this part of town, but he'd come here anyway.

My mother went to the boxes and sank down beside them. She was hushing the chickens now. I went to stand near her and asked what had happened. The Muslim doctor's wife had died. Before she passed, she'd told her husband to send the chickens to my mother as a gift.

How can I take something from her? my mother said. *I gave her nothing.*

She must have believed that you had.

I remembered the look on the doctor's wife's face when she saw the yarn my mother had brought her. It had most certainly been a gift as well.

I opened the boxes so the chickens could be freed into the yard. They squawked and scattered. These chickens weren't brown like ours; they were a pale gray color, and the rooster was beautiful and fierce. When my grandmother waved her skirts at him, he didn't hide under the house, but instead he faced her, a king of roosters, even though he was in a brand-new yard.

Look, I said to my mother.

There were eggs inside the boxes.

My mother reached inside for the eggs. They were not brown like the eggs of our chickens, but a clear lake-colored blue. Something beautiful. A blue my mother had never used as a dye for her yarn because it could not be duplicated. A gift from a woman who was my mother's friend in spite of the fact that they lived in different worlds.

My mother covered her mouth with her hands. She did this whenever she was about to cry, so her spirit couldn't escape from her body in times of sorrow.

My grandmother grabbed my arm and nodded for me to follow her.

Let your mother be, she said. *In losing a friend, she is reminded of all she has lost and all she stands to lose again. There is nothing to be done to make it any easier.*

We all grieve alone.

MY GRANDFATHER'S study was in the cellar, an old cave over which our house had been built. One night I heard cries from that room. I went down the stairs in my nightclothes. My mother and my grandmother were both asleep, but my grandfather was not alone. I looked through a crack in the wooden door that led to the study. I saw my grandfather and Señor deLeon, Friar deLeon's father. There was another man on the table, and he was bleeding; my grandfather was stitching him up with a needle and thread, just as if the man were nothing more complicated than a shirt or a cloak.

I tried to be as quiet as I could. Now I understood; my grandfather was not only a teacher, he was a surgeon, and that was not allowed. All surgery books and medical books had been burned. Having such volumes was almost as bad as having Hebrew books. I felt a shiver go through me and I hurried upstairs. I thought about questions that Catalina had asked me. Why did people come and go from my house in the middle of the night? What were the meetings my grandfather held?

He's a teacher, I had told her.

Catalina had looked suspicious. *Teachers don't teach in the middle of the night.*

Now I wanted to find out the answer to that

question myself. We were not just Marranos; everything my grandfather did and believed was against the church edicts.

When my grandfather came upstairs, he had blood on his clothes. Señor deLeon and the other man had left through the garden door. My grandfather had expected a sleeping house, and I startled him so badly that he dropped everything he was carrying in a clean cloth—knives, thread, needles, things that looked like little axes and little saws, a vial of the bitter liquid that was so strong a person's life could end if he swallowed too much of this elixir for pain.

Get me some water, my grandfather said to me, and I did what he asked.

We stared at each other, and my grandfather said nothing. But when I went to leave, he nodded for me to sit down. My hands and legs were shaking. I pretended we had sat like this together every day of our lives. I sat there politely.

You were downstairs? My grandfather said.

I nodded.

What did you see? he asked then.

Nothing, I told him. *Because nothing is what you*

wanted me to see, though the man on the table might disagree.

My grandfather looked surprised. I had managed to tell the truth while admitting nothing.

Good answer, he said.

My grandfather got up and cleaned his hands with brown soap over the washing bowl. Then he came back to sit across from me.

How much do you know about who you really are? my grandfather asked me.

I know nothing because that is what I'm supposed to know, though my grandmother might disagree.

My grandfather nodded. I had pleased him in some way, without even trying.

Good answer, he said once again.

We were silent for a while; then I told him what I thought.

Maybe a hundred years ago our people should have run away from this place, I said. It was a bold, maybe even rude thing to say, but I had been thinking about this a great deal.

And then run from the next place and the next place and the place after that? You run once, what makes you think you won't have to run all the rest of your life?

Good answer, I said.

My grandfather threw his head back and laughed. That surprised me more than anything. That he could laugh. So I dared to say the next thing to him.

But there are other answers.

My grandfather looked at me as though he'd never seen me before, and maybe he hadn't. He nodded and gave me another answer.

We live moment to moment, my grandfather told me. *Everything changes. One minute we are part of the river, and the next we are joined with the sea.*

If you can stitch a man together with a needle and thread, isn't that magic?

It's medicine. Surgery.

I've heard people say the Jews have magic schools.

It's our way of reaching out to understand the mysteries of God. It's called Kabbalah. *It is the way to learning the way to be one with the world. The way of light and of knowledge.*

The ten gates that lead to the garden, I said. *The ten mysteries of the Tree of Life.*

Who told you that? More than surprise now. Shock that I should know such things. *Your mother?*

I dreamt about them. I thought you might have books that dealt with such things in that room.

What room are you talking about? I thought you saw nothing.

My grandfather was hiding the fact that he had a smile inside him, but I saw it.

True enough. I was just thinking about what I could see, if I ever did see anything. I smiled right back.

You're a smart girl, my grandfather said. *Smarter than I thought you were.*

He took me to see the room downstairs.

Just so you know, he said.

He opened the door with a metal key that was hidden under the last stair. The room was small and filled with books. From the floor to the ceiling. I had not known so many books existed, let alone in our house. This was where he taught his students. On a desk were notes concerning the *Zohar,* the radiant book, the Book of Splendour, the book of true knowledge, a guide to the gates.

What will you say if anyone ever asks you if you've been inside this room? my grandfather asked.

I thought of all the learning that had gone on here, right under my feet. I thought of the people who had been stitched together and healed. I felt something about my grandfather I hadn't felt before. I understood why his students looked at him the way they did.

What room? I said.

I knew it was a good answer; I didn't need anyone to tell me that. Good enough to make Jose deMadrigal, the greatest teacher our town had known, look at me with different eyes.

Sit down, my grandfather told me. *We'll start with the alphabet.*

THERE WAS a quiet in town, but the quiet was like the silence before a torrential downpour. Too still. Too unnatural. Even the birds didn't sing.

On Sunday, at mass, the Friar spoke about how we must have faith in heaven but how we also must be prepared to deal with the evil on earth. I looked around at the people in our congregation. I saw that we were all the same. Marranos. Our truest selves were hidden. And I saw more: We were all frightened. We knew that bad things came together, one after the other, and that some secrets could never be kept. My grandfather had begun to whisper some of these secrets. He taught me about *el Diva del Pardon,* the Day of Pardon, when we atoned for our sins, and about Queen Esther, for whom I had been named, a queen who hid her Jewish heritage to save her people.

I studied with my grandfather nearly every day. I'd always thought I was foolish, yet somehow I learned. There were basic prayers, and there was the radiant way. The way to clear the inside of your head; with chanting, it was possible to bring oneself closer to the all-knowing and all-powerful God. I began to understand that the deeper you looked inside yourself, the more you saw what was infinite and eternal.

One day my grandfather called me to him, there in his study beneath the house. He had been up all night, and his face was pale. His eyes were damp and red. He locked the door and took out some papers. I felt as though the books lining the shelves in his study were alive, breathing, fluttering like doves. I thought I was there to study, but my grandfather kept the books closed.

If anything happens, there are things I want you to

know, he said. He handed me a piece of paper with a name and address. *This man in Amsterdam can help you get onto a boat.*

I nearly laughed. *I don't know where Amsterdam is. I'm here to learn Hebrew. Give this paper to Luis, or to my mother.*

You'll be the one who goes.

Right away, the feeling of laughter left me.

My grandfather was teaching me about the most powerful book, the way of All Light, the Zohar, ideas he said I would not begin to understand until I was a very old woman, and even then they would still be a mystery.

I have chanted all night long, and now I see what the answer is. It will be you, my grandfather said.

No, I said. *It won't be.*

Nothing is easy in this world, my grandfather said. *That's why there are ten gates to pass through before you reach the garden. If life were easy there would be one gate. There would be no gates at all.*

What are the gates made of? I asked.

Crown, Wisdom, Intelligence, Love, Judgment, Compassion, Endurance, Majesty, Foundation of the World, Kingdom.

In my dreams, they seem real, I told my grandfather.

They are made of whatever and however you see them. The gates are always different, but the garden is always the same. And the Tree of Life that grows there is truth. It's joining with the force that is the heart of everything. You name the gates, then you go through them. You walk right through if you are able. He looked right at me. *If you dare.*

SOON AFTER, a letter came from my brother. I had never received a letter before. I had to go down to the Duke's palace and officially sign for it. I paid the soldier in charge of posting letters a few coins to thank him. I went to the well and sat on the edge. My grandfather had sent Luis a coded message telling him that I was now my grandfather's student, even if I was only a girl.

My brother could not write much in his letter; someone at the seminary or in the Duke's palace might decide to open it up and read it. But he told me he was proud of me. He told me our path was dangerous and true and that the most important thing of all was to remember the history of our people.

Every time someone forgets, someone else disappears, my brother wrote.

When I finished reading his letter, I took it home and burned it in a ceramic bowl. That was the best way to keep a secret. Keep it inside your head.

The burning singed the white-and-blue design of the bowl, but to me the pattern looked more beautiful.

What have you done to my bowl! my grandmother cried when she saw the burn marks.

Those are my brother's words burned into it, I told her.

Instead of punishing me, my grandmother used the bowl to serve our dinner. It was adafina, chicken and dumplings, my favorite supper and my brother's favorite as well.

THAT NIGHT, I had a dream about Catalina. I was on one side of a gate, and she was on the other. She was looking for me, calling out my name, but I didn't answer. She was falling; all I had to do was reach out to her to save her, and yet I didn't. This time the gate was made of black feathers, and I knew if I moved, the entire gate might fall apart, that's how fragile it was. So I stayed where I was, silent.

All that day I felt terrible about my dream. Catalina and I no longer went together to the well on the Plaza on Fridays. I decided to go look for her. Maybe I could make things right. I took the wooden buckets in the yard and went to the Plaza. It was not as crowded as it had been before the riots, but there were people coming and going. At the well there was a group of girls my age. Catalina was among them.

As I approached, Catalina spied me. She turned her face away. One of the other girls, Rosa, nudged Catalina. They both looked at me and laughed.

Did you want something? Catalina asked as I approached the well. *There are no pearls to be found in this water. For that you have to go to the seaside.*

I was looking for you, I said.

Well, don't bother. Andres isn't with me.

The girl named Rosa hid her face, but I heard her laughter.

Not him. You, I said.

Well, now that you've found me, you'd better run home. Otherwise I might slap your face. Andres is an idiot. You think you're so much better than I am!

I don't think I'm better than you, I said as I let the buckets down into the well. I drew them up quickly, so that much of the waters splashed out.

Good, Catalina said. *I don't think you are either. I don't know what you are. You don't even cross yourself the way we do.*

I looked up from the well and saw the way Catalina was staring at me. It was late in the day and the sun was huge. I thought about the man with the red circle on his clothes. I thought about the way things burned and disappeared into the air.

As I reached for the water buckets, I could see our reflections in the deep water, floating. There was my friend and there was I.

I saw quite clearly, we looked nothing alike.

———·◆·———

WHAT IF I wasn't who you thought I was? I said to Andres later when we met.

We were beneath the olive tree, the special one. It was late at night, and we were supposed to be in our houses, sleeping. Instead we were here, dreaming out loud. We had sneaked out, and it felt as though we were alone in the world. But we were not.

You are, Andres said. *You're the girl I've been waiting for.*

At this hour, there were creatures in the field I'd never seen in the daytime. Bats, quick little mice, the nightingale I'd heard during the daylight hours, still singing a mournful song.

Maybe I'm not even who I thought I was, I said.

You can be anything at all and it won't matter to me.

How many men had said that to how many women in this world? How many girls had believed such things, only to be left waiting in a doorway?

But sometimes a hawk is a hawk and a dove is a dove and a nightingale is a bird that sings until morning. I decided to trust him.

You won't change your mind? I said.

He laughed and said, *Will you?*

Let me tell you who I really am, I began.

You don't have to. I know you. I know your heart. That's the only thing that will ever matter to me.

I told him anyway. Even though it was dangerous, even though I knew I must never tell. When I was done, he kissed me.

So I gave him my promise, and he did the same, just like that. No matter who we might be in the eyes of anyone else, we belonged to each other.

HUSKS

Who Betrays You

Blood

It was something small that made it happen. Small like the bite of a poisonous bug. That small thing was a kiss.

You would think a kiss could bring only good things into the world, but not this time.

Andres and I continued to meet nearly every night under the olive tree where the hawk had been. It was our secret place.

But secrets can be kept for only so long. I have learned that now.

Catalina caught us. She waited in her yard, and when we met she confronted us. It was a dark night, but there wasn't enough darkness to make this right. Catalina wanted us to explain ourselves.

She felt it was her right to accuse us because she was the wronged party.

We didn't mean for it to happen, I said.

Catalina laughed a hard laugh.

Andres tried to make her understand. *You and I are like brother and sister,* he told her. *My love for you is there,* he explained, *but it's different than the way I feel about Estrella.*

I don't want your love, Catalina told him. Then she turned on me. *I wish I'd never met you. I wish you'd never existed. Now I wonder what else you've lied to me about.*

She closed her eyes as though I had already disappeared. When she opened them again I knew she no longer saw me. I was nothing to her.

THE OFFICIALS didn't come to Catalina. She went to them. She asked for an audience with the judge who was in charge of the court inside the Duke's palace. She knelt before him and told him my grandfather had a secret life and a magic school; that we practiced witchcraft and Judaizing. She told them so easily, she might have been telling him the names of the pigs in her yard.

She did it as though turning us in to the court was the simplest thing, a household chore, a recitation of a daily prayer.

Catalina said that she had seen my grandfather place a spot of blood on our door on the day when known Jews celebrated Passover. When I asked my grandfather if this was true, he said people from our church did so, but it was the blood of chicken, not, as Catalina had said, human blood, the blood of a stolen child.

Catalina told the judge she had never seen anyone in our family eat chorizo, and that brought on her initial suspicions. We refused sausage and roasts, and our pigs were our pets; she announced that we slept in bed with them. She had once heard my grandfather call my grandmother Sarah, when Señora deMadrigal went by the name of Carmen to the rest of town.

And that's what the evidence came down to.

A name.

IT WAS FRIAR DELEON who told us all of this. How Catalina had been escorted out of the old palace as though she were an important person, how she'd been dressed in silk, wearing new satin shoes.

The Friar told us we should leave our town, go without questions and leave everything behind, but the soldiers came so quickly we barely had time to catch our breath. When they arrested my grandfather, they made sure to take everything they needed as evidence for the trial. This meant anything that mattered to us. Our candlesticks, our silver, letters written from my father to my mother, even my box of trinkets from beneath my mattress, in which I kept my pearls.

Luckily, my mother had thought to hide her emerald ring in her shoe. The soldiers took almost everything else and nearly destroyed our house. Dishes shattered, furniture split in two, woven blankets torn apart. My grandmother came at one of the soldiers with a knife, but he just pushed her away and she fell to the ground. The soldier wasn't afraid of her the way I always had been. He barely even saw her.

Don't fight with him, my grandfather said.

We obeyed my grandfather, even though we wept as we did so. At least the soldiers knew nothing about the hidden room filled with books and surgical tools, and they took only one member of our family, because he was the one who'd been said to be an enemy of the church.

The soldier in charge had the decency to let the great teacher Jose deMadrigal walk out the door a free man, but he remained so just until he reached the end of the yard. Then they put irons on him, the heavy sort, used for heretics and murderers.

We were crying and screaming for him, the family of a man for whom there was no hope. We cried so many tears the air itself had turned blue. *Grandfather, father, husband, dearest man.*

The soldiers took our sheep from which my mother had made such fine yarn. The chickens scattered and hid under the house, but the pigs were herded together, out the gate, down the lane, following behind my grandfather. At the very last moment, one of the soldiers grabbed Dini, my pet, and carried him away over his shoulder. Dini was screaming and he sounded like a person. I tried to go after him, but my mother ran to me and held me back; she covered my ears. All the same I could hear what the soldiers were doing;

I could see it even when I closed my eyes. My grandfather, my pet, my life, my world. I knew the monster on the Plaza had walked through our house, destroying everything.

We stood there, broken.

FRIAR DELEON came again that evening to tell us we should leave. Leave my grandfather. Leave our home.

Now I began to understand why there were people who decided to stay. It was not so easy to abandon those you loved.

When we refused to run, the Friar told us we must stay away from the courthouse. I promised I would go no farther than the yard, but even while I said so, I had another plan entirely. I'd seen what had happened to the Arrias family; I knew my grandfather's trial was to begin.

The next morning, I told my mother and grandmother I was going to the fields behind our house. Instead, I made my way to the Plaza, wearing a shawl over my head so no one would recognize me. I hid everything but my eyes. I sneaked in at the last moment, before the court doors closed, and sat in the back.

I recognized someone a few rows in front of me. I knew her from the shape of her head, from the rise of her shoulders, from the way she clasped her hands and rested them on the bench in front of her. Catalina.

How had I never noticed how hard Catalina was, how brightly she shone when something bad was happening to someone else? She had watched us: my beautiful mother, my strong grandmother, my brilliant brother, and she'd been dull with jealousy. So dull I hadn't seen what was shining beneath her skin. She was green with it; I saw that now. She would not be called as a witness; only the judge would speak. All the same, Catalina was at the center of the trial, and she knew it; she was shining like an emerald. She had styled her hair carefully and put it up with tortoise-shell combs. I wondered if those combs had come from some Marrano woman who'd been stripped of everything she owned.

A long list of crimes was read out at last. *Heresy, judaizing, magic, medicine, murder, blood.*

They called my grandfather a sorcerer. The greatest sorcerer of our town and of our times. The most evil, the most dangerous, an even bigger threat to the townspeople than the black fever had been.

The court decided to test my grandfather. I had heard of such tests. They were like holding a witch's head underwater to see if she would drown. Only her death could prove her innocence; a circle of impossible, deathly judgment.

They brought out a sausage made of Dini, and they made this announcement: It had come from a pig that had lived for three years without being cooked. A pig that had slept in bed with the women of the family.

People in the courtroom let loose with their disgust, cursing us, damning us, we who had become less than human. Marranos. Pigs.

As for me, I felt something rise in my throat: the horror of the world of men.

MY GRANDFATHER refused to eat the sausage. He said he was sick. He said he could not eat anything. He said he believed this court was unjust, and that the outcome of every trial would suit the judge and not the truth.

The guards opened his mouth and forced the sausage in. When my grandfather spat it out, they forced it back in, only this time they clamped his mouth shut with a metal mask. They tightened the mask until we could hear the bones in his face break, even in the back row. They told my grandfather he would be released when he'd finished eating the pig. After a while he nodded, but when they unlatched the mask, he spit it at them again. I saw the end of his life right there in that single moment. His pride, his decency, his secrets, his death.

The court officials had brought in a rabbi from the juderia in order to question him. I recognized him; he was the old man with the beard whose books had been burned. He still wore the red circle on his vest. In the back of the court were two women dressed in black with that same circle sewn to their clothes. I looked at them, then looked away. I recognized the language they spoke. *Ladino.* A mixture of Hebrew and Spanish;

the language my grandparents spoke to each other when they believed no one was listening.

I felt the world that I knew tumbling away from me. The judge asked the rabbi if my grandfather was a Judaizer, practicing the rites of Jewry. Question after question came. Was he known to be a surgeon? Did he own books? Did he run a magic school? The rabbi said *no* to each question in a sharp voice. His voice was hard and seemed to be coming from a far distance away. He had raven eyes, dark and deep. He spoke with a raven's voice, old and wise and far above the cruelty of the human race.

The rabbi did not want to answer the court; still, they questioned him. Was my grandfather a sorcerer, known to practice from books of magic and illumination? Could he take people apart and put them back together with a needle and thread? Did he chant during the new moon and during fasting times?

The rabbi looked at my grandfather. Over a hundred years earlier some had stayed and some had fled. Some had been forced into the juderia, where they'd been brutalized; others went to Portugal or Amsterdam; still others went underground and practiced their beliefs in secret. What difference did it make? There was no red circle on my grandfather's clothes, true enough, but now the worst crime was pretending to be something you were not.

If this was true, what did it mean about Catalina—she who pretended to be my friend and was the opposite instead? When I looked at her, she appeared to be a different person from the one I'd known. My friend had disappeared into green smoke. And now I saw that the court had given her a gift for her betrayal.

Catalina was wearing my pearls.

She had rewritten everything, our history together, our friendship. Now I was the girl who'd stolen Andres; the girl who'd lied to her about who I was. Therefore, she owed me nothing.

To get my grandfather to speak, they arrested my mother. Catalina's mother had joined her daughter to offer the evidence against her; she'd told the judges that my mother laid eggs, like a hen. Blue eggs that were filled with human blood.

There had been a drought, and we had no rain-water in our barrel; because my mother would not allow me to go for water, the guards arrested her while she was at the well in the center of the Plaza. Where the water had come directly from heaven. Where my family had come to drink for over five hundred years.

They dragged her away by her hair. That is what our neighbor Señora dePaz had run to our house to tell us. When I went to search for my mother there were strands of her hair everywhere. Birds were gathering in the Plaza, a thousand fluttering doves, each with a strand of black hair in its beak.

The soldiers had dragged my mother over the cobblestones. My grandmother and I were both there, in the back row, when Abra was brought into court that same afternoon; there were still red bloody bands running down her face, her arms, her legs.

And there was Catalina—only one row away.

The judge first asked my mother if she could cure a cold. Like the rabbi with the red circle, she should have said *no* to everything. She should have become a raven. She didn't understand that every word the judge said was a trap, and that every word she said could easily be a stone used to shut her into that trap.

My mother said it was a simple enough thing to cure a cold with a mixture of garlic and root teas. We could all tell from the judge's face that this was the wrong answer. The next question came: Could she make a baby come before its time? She could do so if necessary, if the mother was ill or the baby so big it needed to enter into our world early – she made an elixir of roots and leaves and had the mother-to-be walk all around until dawn, preferably on the first night of a full moon.

My mother sat there calmly; she didn't understand how she had stumbled into the judge's snare until he began the next series of accusations. The judge's face was still expressionless, as if he were a reasonable man and this were a reasonable proceeding.

Could she call fallen angels to do her bidding? Could she murder with a curse and a bit of blood smeared on the door? Could she seduce men by saying their names backwards a dozen times; could the mark of the devil be found in her left eye; could she lay eggs like a hen, and were those eggs indeed filled with blood? Did she, as witches and Jews were said to do, sleep with pigs in her bed?

My mother had stopped speaking. The trap had closed over her, and there was nothing she could do. You cannot disprove the ridiculous. You cannot argue reasonably with evil.

Abra deMadrigal did not look young enough to be my sister anymore. Her sorrow weighed her down and aged her. She was still beautiful, but she looked very far away. No wonder our people had raven eyes, so distant, so sad. No matter how wise she was, my mother looked like a woman who hadn't truly believed how much evil there was in our world. Not until this moment.

What I heard in that courtroom seemed like a dream; what I saw, a nightmare. Would I wake up and find the scene before me dissolved into ordinary life? I bit hard into the heel of my hand, until I tasted blood, real blood, human blood. From the way I hurt I knew the truth: There was no waking up from this now.

Andres had heard what had happened when he

came home from working in the fields. He had run to the courthouse to be with me.

You can't be here, Andres told me. *It's too dangerous.*

At first I refused to leave. My grandmother looked over at Andres, surprised to see him.

What is he doing here? she asked me.

Nothing, I assured her. I turned to Andres. *Go.*

Do you think it's over? Andres told me. *My aunt has gone again to speak to the judges. Who knows what lies she'll tell. They'll come for the rest of your family. Raven, they'll come for you.*

When I whispered to my grandmother that we should leave, she waved me away.

You go, she said. *You shouldn't be here. You're a child.*

I went out to the courtyard with Andres, but I wouldn't go any farther. I had to wait for my grandmother and bring her with me.

Andres and I crouched in the shadows, not speaking. We were close enough to feel each other's hearts beating. When the crowd came pouring out of the court, I saw my grandmother limping along, pushed forward in the great swell of people. Andres reached her and helped her toward the shadows.

I told my grandmother that we were going into the woods, where we could be safe for the night. My grandmother pulled away. She insisted she had to go back to her house; she had to clean for when my grandfather came home.

Andres and I looked at each other. My grandmother was overwhelmed by what was happening to us. She had moved back into the past because the here and now was too terrible. I was gentle with my grandmother, as if she were the child, not I. I told my grandmother she could clean the next day and that I would help her. But by now I understood: We were never going to live in our house again. For all I knew the soldiers were waiting for us already.

We got out of town as quickly as we could. Halfway up the hillside that led to the woods, my grandmother collapsed. She said she couldn't go any farther. She had to go back to see my mother and grandfather; she had to have the house clean and ready; she had to stay in her bed chamber and lock all the doors.

You have to go on, Andres said. *Otherwise Estrella will follow you back to town, and if she does she'll be taken, too. Is that what you want?*

My grandmother looked at Andres as though she had never seen him before.

I'll protect you both, he said. *We'll protect each other.*

THEY KILLED MY GRANDFATHER that night. While my grandmother and I were sleeping in a meadow, they beat him to death with stones. They broke his bones one by one. They tried to make him confess his sins, and he refused. Andres found this out from a farmer when he went to an orchard to buy fruit and cheese for our breakfast. People all over town had listened for my grandfather's cries, but there were none. Only silence.

When I told my grandmother what had happened, she held up her hand to stop me. She didn't want to hear.

Do not speak of your grandfather again until we are in his presence, she told me.

My grandmother seemed half the size she used to be. Saying a single sentence took most of her strength. All around her was a puddle of blue liquid. Just as my mother had told me. The color of tears.

Andres thought it was his duty to protect us, but I wanted to protect him also. No matter how much it might hurt.

It's not safe for you to stay with us, I told him on the day my grandfather died.

I don't care, Andres said.

Well, then, I don't want you here.

He looked at me, hurt. Still, I went on. Sometime a lie was told in the best interest of someone you loved.

Go now, I said.

Promise me one thing: You won't go back to town, he said to me.

There were no longer any promises worth keeping.

Don't come into the woods anymore, I told him. *Forget the way. Forget me.*

I turned so I didn't have to see him leave, but I knew when he was gone. I kept my eyes shut until there was silence, until I could no longer hear him walking away.

THE NEXT DAY, I told my grandmother I was going to search for food, but that was another lie. I made sure she had water and that she was comfortable, then I went into town. I wore my shawl over my head. I needed to go see my mother. I didn't care if it wasn't safe; nothing was anymore.

I wasn't the only one outside the wall of the prison. There were dozens of people there, all calling out the name of their son or daughter or husband. All losing someone they loved.

In the Plaza, a bonfire was being built. I could smell green wood; it burned my nose when I breathed in.

Why are they doing that? I asked a man next to me.

I had never seen a bonfire that tall.

Everyone in this prison will be burned for heresy, my neighbor at the wall told me. *They'll burn in agony.*

I saw my mother at a window, her face peering through the metal bars. I felt that I was staring into a pool, seeing my own reflection. I thought of the bowl of water my mother taught me to look into. It was true, everything a person ever needed to know was right there in a single bowl small enough to fit in the palm of one hand.

My mother saw me. She threw something out the window, and I ran to get it. An old lady got to it before I could. It was a piece of wool with something wrapped inside.

It belongs to my mother! I told the old lady.

Well, now it's mine!

The old lady was there to see what she could buy cheaply from those people desperately trying to sell family treasures in order to buy food and clean water for those they loved who were trapped in prison.

The old lady unwrapped the fabric, greedy, then made a hissing sound. There was only a rotten onion inside.

This is what you want—take it. The old lady threw it to me.

I held the onion in my hands. I did not have to peel it to find I had tears in my eyes. I looked at the window, but my mother was gone. I went down the street and found a place in the shadows.

I sat down and peeled the onion. My mother had made a hole she had patched up with onion skin. Inside was her emerald ring. The one my father gave her when he pledged his love, a lifetime and a world away; it was now her final gift to me.

ONE GIFT deserves another in return. So my mother had taught me, and so I believed.

I went to the Muslim doctor's house in search of a gift for my mother. I had no one else to go to in a time such as this. No one with any power. I had to bang on the door before the yard boy answered, the one who'd brought us the chickens. When I said I needed to see the doctor, the boy shouted at me. We didn't speak the same language; all we could do was shout at each other.

The doctor must have heard us. He came out and waved the boy away. I was afraid the doctor would shout at me, too. But he spoke to me kindly, asking me what I wanted.

Help for my mother, I said.

You think I can do anything in this world?

The doctor looked different than he had when his wife was alive. Ashy. He was wearing the blue

garment his wife had made for him out of my
mother's yarn. I could tell that he'd put it on
when his wife died, and hadn't taken it off.

*My mother helped your wife make something for
you. Now you help me!*

I think I was crying. I sounded angry, but that's
not what I was.

*They've built a bonfire on the Plaza. My mother is
one of the prisoners they intend to burn.*

*I can make her something to help her into the next
world, whatever that is for your people.* The Muslims
called us the People of the Book. He knew who I
was. And still he wanted to help me.

I looked at the doctor. I was standing next to
the red lily, the one that grew from true love.

You understand me? the doctor said. *It's to let her
choose her time so that she flies away before the pain.*

I nodded. I wanted that for my mother. It was
all I could give her now.

Wait here, the doctor said to me.

When the doctor went inside his house, I sat
down beneath an olive tree. The air was so heavy
I felt I might fall asleep. Soon enough, the doctor's boy came out to me. He handed me a pack-

et. Inside, there were two tablets made of white powder. We looked at each other, and then the boy ran away.

I walked through the market, circling the fruit and vegetable bins until I saw a brown onion on the ground. I kicked it in front of me until I could reach down and steal it. I poked a hole into the onion and placed the tablets inside. My mother knew medicine; she was a healer. She would know the tablets were to take her far from this world. To help her fly.

I tried to get back to the prison, but there were soldiers everywhere. A woman who went to our church and who sometimes made almond cakes with my grandmother, Señora Rocamora, grabbed me.

Run away, she told me. *They're looking for you and your brother.*

Thankfully, my brother was safe in the seminary. I asked my grandmother's old friend to bring the onion to my mother, and to throw it over the gate when she saw Abra. The Señora thought she might be too old and weak to throw anything over the prison wall, but before she could make up her mind, I lost her. The crowd started pushing, and in an instant Señora Rocamora was gone, taken by soldiers. The soldiers had come so close to me, I had felt the heat from their bodies. I was wearing my shawl, so that no one would recognize me, but just to make certain, I ran.

When I got back to the woods, Andres was waiting for me. He was watching over my grandmother. He hadn't stayed away as I'd asked.

The truth was, I had never been more grateful to see someone.

As soon as my grandmother fell asleep, Andres and I went far into the woods. It was dark, but we could see by starlight.

So now you know why we can never be together, I told him.

We can't be together here, Andres said. *But this isn't the only place in the world. I'll do anything for you.*

My grandfather had told me I should go to Amsterdam; maybe we could go together. But I couldn't go anywhere yet. I wasn't finished with Encaleflora.

I handed Andres the onion.

If you want to do something for me, take this to the prison and call out my mother's name. When you see her, throw this inside to her. Tell her it's my gift to her.

What else can I do? Andres asked.

He meant it, so I asked for more. I had no pride anymore.

You can try to get word to my brother. Tell him to leave the seminary and go as far away as he can. Tell him to go to Amsterdam.

I'll get word to him to go there, Andres assured me.

Andres didn't come back until very late. He brought us some bread and cheese. My grandmother and I had been starving. He did protect us, as he said he would, this time from hunger. But I knew he'd done much more.

When my grandmother went to sleep, Andres and I went deeper into the woods. I asked if my mother had gotten the onion. She had. Andres had called out for her, and when she came to the window to see who was shouting her name, Andres had thrown her the onion through the bars. Abra quickly hid it inside her clothes. Her hands were still blue from the yarn she'd dyed for so very long. She had cried so many tears, she had no more inside of her.

Thank my daughter, my mother had called. *It is the greatest gift she could have given me.*

ANDRES HAD ALSO gone to see Friar deLeon. At first the Friar refused to speak to him, but when Andres explained that I had sent him, the Friar vowed to get word to my brother if he could. After that, Andres had done one more thing. He had also spoken with a friend who could help to get my grandmother and me to Amsterdam, where we could find the man my grandfather had told me about. From there, we would take a boat to an island so far away, nothing could hurt us.

But it would cost dearly.

I looked at Andres. Just the thought of leaving him stopped me.

I'm going with you, he said.

I took my mother's emerald from the chain on my neck and gave it to him to pay for our passage.

My mother had been right, it was the one thing that lasted, the one thing we could depend on. Other than our love for each other, it was all we had right now.

Earth

I wished that we lived in another time, another country. But maybe that wouldn't have mattered. There comes a time when every one of our people understands that a Jew can never be attached to a place. The rules always change, and we always lose. People will always despise us, and we must be ready to fly away. We cannot have roots in the earth of any country, only in the garden that we carry inside us.

Two days more in the woods, and Andres did not come back.

Three days. Four.

My grandmother said he had taken the emerald and disappeared. She said I was a fool to trust anyone. I kept my thoughts to myself. Andres would never betray me. I knew it as well as my mother had known that my father was her one true love.

My grandmother could not be convinced there was any hope left in our lives. She was pulling out her hair in little clumps. She was whispering prayers I didn't know. She wanted to go home, and even though we had no home anymore, I understood when she said that we needed to go back one more time to look at the place where we'd spent our lives.

So we could remember.

It was dangerous, but I took my grandmother there. What else did she have? What else could I give to her? As I had sent a gift to my mother, I now gave a gift to my grandmother as well.

We went at dusk, wrapped in black shawls. We were like foreigners in our own village. Our house looked as if it had been deserted years ago. The door had been torn off, and the yard was bare, no chickens, no pigs. I refused to think about certain things. My family, my pet Dini, the kitchen table where my great-great-grandmother had kneaded dough for bread.

I left my grandmother to look through the house; I didn't want to step inside.

There was something else I needed to do.

I went to Catalina's house and stood in the yard. I thought about the day when we went to the Plaza, when there were sparks in her hair. I thought of how we had slept in the same bed and whispered our dreams to each other. We had called each other sister.

Instead of knocking on the door, I picked up a stone and threw it as hard as I could. Something shattered. Something broke.

Catalina came to the door and opened it, not all the way, but enough. I could see her.

This isn't what I wanted to happen, she said to me. *But you betrayed me.*

I looked hard to see if she was saying some cruel joke; but, no. She meant it.

You took my cousin, Catalina said.

And then I understood that she had no idea what she'd done to my family. She thought love and hatred were equal.

I tore my clothes the way my grandfather told me our people did to mourn our dead. I did it right there in Catalina's yard, so she could see that she was dead to me. I spoke a curse that my grandmother had taught me:

May you know another's suffering, may you know it all the days of your life, now and forever, until you understand what you have done.

WHEN I WENT to get my grandmother, our neighbor, Señor dePaz, came out of his house, though he clearly was nervous. He stood in the shadows of our house, beneath a trellis of white flowers that still smelled sweet, as they had every summer of my life. The scent of jasmine was everywhere; a deep and tragic scent.

They've brought your brother down from the seminary, the Señor told me. *They sent a dozen soldiers to get him.*

I went into my old house and told my grandmother we had to hurry. I didn't look around, but I did grab for some of the food we had left behind. Olives and stale almond cakes. My grandmother was carrying books that belonged to my grandfather, but I told her she could take only one. She took my grandfather's notebook, in which everything he believed was written, and she carried it close to her heart, inside her shawl.

I'D THOUGHT my brother was safe because he was so far away from home. But nothing in our realm was far enough away. I explained to my grand- mother that if we went to try and see my brother, we risked being caught. We made the decision together. We would go. Neither of us would consider doing otherwise.

By the time my grandmother and I had reached the Plaza, my brother was already tied to a wooden post. There were fifty people tied up, all in agony, including my mother. My brother's heresy was considered to be the worst, because he was studying to be a priest. They had stripped him of his clothes and shaved his head; they had beaten him with thin leather strips, so there wasn't a piece of him that hadn't been cut and scarred. They broke his bones one at a time. My grandfather could never have stitched Luis back together, not if he used all the red thread in the world.

I saw Friar deLeon standing in the crowd. He was weeping, but that wasn't enough for me. I told my grandmother to stay close to the wall, in the shadows. My fierce grandmother nodded her head meekly and did as she was told. I went over to the Friar, and when he saw me he put out his arms to embrace me, but I backed away.

I thought you were supposed to be the champion of your people, I said.

I live because I need to do that. For anyone who is left.

Don't you see? No one will be left. Protect them now or there will be no one to protect!

This is a battle that goes on and on. It never ends. You're too young to understand.

No! You're too much of a coward to fight.

I was sick of lies and secrets and of battles so old we had to erase who we were to fight back. And still we lost. Still we were tied to posts.

THE GUARDS poured water on the leather straps, and in the hot sun the straps grew tighter and tighter until they forced blood to stream out of people's eyes and mouths. Some good people in the Plaza were praying, Christians and Jews and Muslims. But there were many in that crowd who wanted blood. The monster from deep inside the earth was crawling along the Plaza. The monster had been formed from burning books and smoke and hate, but it had grown so big and strong, it could reach up and ring the bell in the chapel of the old Duke's house. The bell kept ringing and ringing, and the people kept screaming, and there was no way to stop it.

MAYBE I'D thrown that stone through Catalina's window so she would have to hear the voices of the accused. She couldn't shut them out now. People could hear the victims crying miles and miles away. If Catalina lived to be a hundred years old, she would still hear them, even when she'd grown deaf, when she couldn't hear anything else.

People were laughing at my mother. They said if she was so good at magic, if she'd learned so much from her father the sorcerer, why didn't she save herself now? Why didn't she become a bird or a snake? I hoped she had swallowed the tablets I'd brought her from the Muslim doctor. He said she would fly like a bird when she swallowed it; she would be above the world looking down at a world of snakes.

And then I realized she had done nothing of the sort. I looked at my brother and saw his eyes were closed. My mother had managed to get the tablets to him. Luis was no longer feeling anything. They couldn't hurt him anymore; his spirit had moved above him, even though his body was still breathing its last ragged breaths.

I spoke to Luis without speaking. I said a prayer that no one could hear. My lips moved quickly.

I knew that my brother would still be a part of this world no matter what happened next. I felt my love for him so deeply that my blood seemed to flow down the street to him. My blood sang out my prayer for Luis even while he was still living in our world.

My grandmother had made her way across the Plaza to find me. I told her to turn away when they lit the fire with their torches. Everything smelled rotten: blood and sweat and filth. The way evil smelled. I could not understand how something so horrible could be in the world, the deeds of men such as these. They were using green wood. Green wood burns so long it lasts an eternity. It smells green as it sputters and smokes, but it is the worst of deaths. That was what they wanted: suffering. They gave to us all eternity to cry for what we lost.

Because my mother was so beautiful, the judge took pity on her. He had the sentry garrote her, breaking her neck before the fire reached her so she would not feel the flames. That was the judge's idea of pity. I thought I heard my mother gasp when they killed her, even from so far away. I thought I saw her spirit escape and fly upward.

Fifty people were set on fire.

And then the screaming really began. Like cold knives, like a storm, like the cries of the angels who come to earth to avenge all evil. The fire was so hot we could feel it, like a wave that pushed against us. There were so many red sparks in the air we swallowed them through our veils. The hem of my grandmother's dress caught fire, and I had to stamp out the flames. My grandmother stood still and did nothing. If it had been up to her, she would have burned along with the others.

My grandmother was crying beside me. I had never seen her cry, and I couldn't look at her now. I'd been so afraid of her my whole life, and now she was afraid. I could not bear to see it. My grandmother was wearing the black scarf, as I was. No one noticed us. We were covered head to foot in ashes; two women made of ashes ready to be blown apart, carried to all the corners of the world, east and west alike.

There was so much screaming, it was nearly impossible to think. People ran and tried to get to their loved ones. As soon as they did, they were struck down, some of them killed, bleeding, their heads opened up on the cobblestones. Nothing could change this now. It was a stone rolling down a hill, getting bigger and bigger, unstoppable, taking down everything in its path.

The fire was out of control. People were choking on the sparks and the smoke. One of the guards breathed in fire, then clutched at his throat and chest as he lay dying. I knew we had to back away from the heat. We had to disappear from that place. But how could I leave my brother? I looked up; through the flames I could see him.

I know this is true: He opened his eyes for an instant. Other people were writhing and melting, but my brother stopped his flight long enough to look at me. An instant that would have to last forever. And then the flames rose higher and my brother was gone.

The smoke was so black it was like a storm cloud.

Forever after the well water that had come from heaven would be black, filled with ashes.

Sky

I pulled my grandmother toward the Muslim quarter, along the narrow streets that smelled like cinnabar and sweet bay. I felt that dove inside myself, beating inside my skin, in a panic. I thought the quarter might be the only place where my grandmother and I could disappear. We wrapped our shawls over our heads; with our dark features, we looked like anyone else on the street. But we brought the smell of fire with us, on our clothes, in our hair. Some men yelled at us. We ran faster. Maybe they were saying we were bad luck. Maybe they were saying women shouldn't be out alone as night approached.

I went to the only address I knew. The doctor's house. It was dusk, and I dragged my grandmother along. It was getting more difficult. She was as heavy as a person who had given up; she resisted every step, but when I pulled hard enough, she followed, like a sack of ashes that hadn't enough life and will to disobey.

There were no lamps burning in the doctor's house and no patients at his door. When my mother and I used to come here, the chickens would put up a fuss; now the yard was silent. I thought of the chickens that had belonged to the doctor's wife, scattered now, roaming our neighborhood until they were caught by Catalina's mother or someone else. Whoever stole them would be surprised at the color of the eggs they collected the next morning. Surely they would wonder if blue eggs were a blessing or a curse. When they cracked them open, there would be human blood inside; it was true. My mother's blood that would last forever after. The blood of my brother, my grandfather, my father.

I wished whoever cooked those eggs and ate them would choke. I knew a curse you make always stays with you, but I didn't care. I myself would never eat eggs again. Not even if there were nothing else to eat other than weeds and stones.

WE SNEAKED into the doctor's stable. No one would find us here; we could be safe for a night. There was a mule that wasn't happy to see us; he hee-ed and hawed till I gave him some of the almond cakes I'd put in my pockets. Then the mule followed me and wouldn't leave me alone. He had warm breath and dark eyes, and I thought about Dini. I thought about how he meant so much to me and meant nothing to the soldiers who took him. I thought about how Dini had followed me and knew when I was upset; how he'd been faithful in some way most people could not even imagine.

I could not bring myself to think of all that the soldiers had done. If I thought about all the horrible things in the world, I would end up like my grandmother. A sack of ashes. As good as dead. Defying whatever days were granted to me, throwing them away as though I were a helpmate to those who wanted to destroy us.

My grandmother wasn't talking. She was

wrapped in her shawl, unmoving, as though ready to be buried. My mother had whispered that our people are always buried simply, ready to join the eternal, wrapped in a white shroud and quickly placed into the earth. Everyone is made from dust and everyone returns to it. That is what she told me, and that was what I believed. In my mind, I wrapped my mother and my brother and my grandfather in white cloth. I closed my eyes and put them in the ground under an almond tree, in a place where there was always water.

When I offered my grandmother a bit of stale cake, she waved me away. She said there was no point to anything, least of all eating. She said this world was a hole of darkness, of black light and evil and loss.

But if that were true, there would never have been any bright light in our lives. My mother would never have existed, my brother would never have been such a fine man, Andres would not be waiting for me somewhere, though I didn't know where.

I told my grandmother she was wrong. We had to survive to remember. Otherwise everything we were would disappear. Those people we loved would fade as though we'd never loved them, as if they'd never walked and talked and burned. Forgetting them was the real evil. That was the hole of darkness.

I found a cup and took water from the mule's trough and insisted that my grandmother drink. When she was done, I made a bed for her out of an old rug. I went to stand outside when she was asleep. I looked at the swirls of stars. They were the same stars I'd always seen and might not see again once we left this place.

The doctor came outside to say his nighttime prayers. He was still wearing the blue coat his wife had made out of my mother's yarn, spun from the sheep in our yard, dyed with flowers from the hills above us. He prayed beside the red flower, proof of eternal love.

The doctor acted as if he didn't see me, but he knew I was there. After he prayed he said, *It is fine for you to sleep in the stable. But leave in the morning while it's still dark. That way the soldiers will not find you.*

I thanked him for his kindness. *I think that red*

lily will always grow, I said. I wanted to honor his wife in some way.

As I was leaving to return to the stable, I heard him say, *Now we both have people we love who are like birds. They have flown far from anything in this world that can hurt them. They're flying away still.*

I THOUGHT about how the soldiers had burned the books first. How the pages were like doves. Everything we knew condemned us, and our questioning condemned us most of all. Knowledge was the way of our people, and knowledge was dangerous. It was the thing that freed you and the thing that put you in peril. It was the key to the ten gates. I saw them clearly now, each and every one, the gates that were there for me. *Ashes, Bones, Grass, Heart, Stone, Love, Sorrow, Blood, Earth, Sky.*

JUST BEFORE DAYLIGHT, my grandmother and I went back to the hills. We did not get there till late at night. Andres was waiting for us with two mules. I knew he wouldn't betray me. I felt that there was hope for us somewhere in the world.

We would go to Amsterdam, where there was the boat waiting. We were going to a place so far away, no one would follow us. We were going to an island made of stones on the other side of the ocean. Hispañola. We would fit in there because we spoke Spanish; but we would not be like everyone else. On Friday nights, as the sky darkened, as the clouds moved out to sea, far past the island, past the shore and the stones, we would light candles and say our prayers, and no one would stop us. At last we could be who we really were. Some people say, *Save yourself and you save your life.* I say, *Be yourself and you save your soul.*

ANDRES WAITED while my grandmother and I followed the path my mother had shown me. When we reached the pool, we took off our filthy ash-coated clothes. I saw my grandmother as the girl she once had been and the old woman she had become. I helped her into the bath and then I let myself slip into the dark water.

It was so clear and so clean, as though the pool had come directly from heaven. The stars were caught in the water, like embers. Where we were going, there would be different stars in the sky, so I wanted to remember these, the ones floating in our heaven-water, the ones I'd known all my life.

Even when I was an old woman, older than my grandmother, older than the oldest raven in the sky, I'd remember everything I'd ever known and seen. The ashes and the burning doves. The look on my brother's face, the blue dye on my mother's hands, the color of tears, the gate of sorrow, and the gate of love.

I'd sit down and make my sons and daughters listen, though we were thousands of miles away, far on another shore.

Remember what I've told you.

Remember me.